PRETERNATURAL
BOOK 2
EVOLUTION

Welcome Back...

PETER TOPSIDE

Contents

Welcome Back

Meadowsville had lived to see another day, but fifteen years after Blackheart was defeated, the town still was under his control. His presence never disappeared, even while his cold body lay buried up on Chrysanthemum Drive. Blackheart's soul and spirit would always be a part of Meadowsville, and there was no hope in that changing. Even the cool breeze on this early spring day felt like a monster breathing on someone's neck, preparing to feed on their body and soul, sending the uncertainty of their mortality into a tailspin.

The sun rose, eliminating the shadows and darkness that were once the highlight of this place and bringing a bright beam of light that exposed the new problems of this once prosperous town. Houses that once had been a sight to behold now appeared worn and shoddy, even abandoned. Fewer cars traveled the now pothole-marked roads. Many of the former businesses were boarded up and advertising cheap lease rates. The remaining townsfolk all bore a similar resemblance to one another, appearing decades older than they should. Meadowsville was a shell of its former self.

Ever since the town saw the demise of its popularity from the Mr. Smith legend, many residents moved away in search of jobs and income. The remaining people were barely able to scrape by each month but tried to remain loyal to their once beautiful and immaculate town. The transition had been very difficult, but the newly elected, optimistic, and honorable mayor, Chazz Wiggins, had brought new hope. As a lifelong resident, he wanted to do his part and help his hometown become a thing of beauty once again, not just for his eventual family but for all his fellow citizens.

Elected several months prior, he had fired the last remaining department heads who had served under his predecessors and the former Mayor Wilkins and appointed his own handpicked people he had grown up with. Though a huge undertaking, with the right leadership, the town's slow progression into a stable and profitable economy was only a matter of time.

Christian Reed was praised as the hero of Meadowsville after his heroic actions battling Blackheart. He was given a medal of courage, customized tactical armor, and permission by the township to patrol each night to ensure everyone's safety. While most of the community still respected him and his public service, there was a growing trend of distaste aimed at him. Everyone had tried to move on, and he served as one of the last remaining symbols of the town's troubled past. His patrols were now viewed as nothing better than when Blackheart would stalk the town each night.

Christian Reed and fellow Meadowsville resident Alexandra Hughes had stayed close, even during her schooling. After witnessing Blackheart's siege on Meadowsville and being the first person to physically harm the legendary monster, Alexandra received no kudos for her efforts in saving the town. It all went to Christian, and part of her was content with not receiving the attention. She didn't want to be constantly reminded of her friend David, and Blackheart, and everything that happened all that time ago, but it was all Christian would talk about during their interactions. He was obsessed, but she couldn't bring herself to ask him to stop. So she let him continue on at her expense.

She had delayed going away to school after her encounter with Blackheart and became a dedicated caregiver to her father. She cooked, cleaned, and helped him in the church. She felt very hollow but saw it as her duty to take on her mother's role to support him.

After several years of this, Father Richard forced her to leave to complete her schooling. She spent all her time away isolated and unable to develop any meaningful friendships. It was just her, her studies, and her guilt as allies during those years.

Christian's wife, Rebecca, checked in with Alex almost daily, mothering and supporting her, which was one of the only things that kept Alexandra going forward. She came back for major holidays but was never there more than a few days at a time—just enough time to see the Reed family, help her father, and then pack up to leave again. She was unable to visit David's memorial stone for a long time after his death at the hands of Blackheart. It was just too much for her to see.

Each time became harder and harder to leave her father, as she noticed his age and slowly declining health. But he instructed her to continue on, despite his ailments, not acknowledging her conflicted feelings.

During her contact with both Christian and Rebecca, she had noticed the Reed family was deteriorating more each time they spoke. Their fifteen-year-old son, Adam, and his mother fought in private about Christian's behavior. Christian barely attended his scheduled therapy sessions and suffered from untreated alcoholism. He took inadequate mood-stabilizing medications and suffered from unresolved trauma, all stemming from losing his firstborn, Caroline, at the hands of David due to Blackheart's manipulation of him. Not a day went by when he didn't vividly remember walking home that faithful night and seeing his only daughter brutalized and bloodied, lying motionless in David's arms. Christian's guilt over her death made him unable to let both himself and the town forget Blackheart, and it antagonized Meadowsville.

Despite her worries and conflicted feelings, Alexandra earned her bachelor's degree and then her master of divinity. Her ambition was to stay away from Meadowsville once her schooling had been completed, but her father became unable to run the church alone. She moved back home after an eight-year hiatus to help him with the Meadowsville Community Church. Seeing the downfall of her hometown in person made her very nostalgic, and she decided to stay there and take over after Father Richard passed away.

To her dismay, Alexandra found she was not able to operate the church without him. Her sermons were mediocre at best, and despite her training, she struggled to be the leader she felt the church needed while also initiating and leading several community outreach programs, all aimed at helping those affected by Blackheart or Mr. Smith.

She had no significant relationships and found she was unable to connect with men in general. This was one of the biggest obstacles she faced, and it fed the overall uncertainty she felt about her life. The memory of David lived on, and she had spent the last fifteen years riddled with grief after he passed. Though their friendship was brief, it had been the most meaningful relationship she'd ever had, aside from her father.

This town was a very different place than before, and the issues the community faced were far from over.

Welcome back to Meadowsville . . .

2

Sermon Attempt

On a pleasant, sunny day, Alexandra stood before her enormous congregation at Meadowsville Community Church. The seventy-five-member congregation had ballooned to almost five hundred, most of whom were regular attendees at the weekly services. The church could handle this type of crowd, but Alexandra, growing up in this same church, was still taken back by the sheer volume. She had never been a great public speaker, and with so many people looking to her for evocative sermons week in and week out, she was unsure which topics to focus on. They all came from different backgrounds, experiences in Meadowsville, and family dynamics, and she tried to find a simple yet effective way to unite them all under God, with her being the mediator for such a momentous act. Finding the proper balance between her studies and their practical applications was crucial for her position, but she critiqued herself constantly rather than allowing time and experience to make her an accomplished and successful leader.

She took a deep breath and quickly reviewed her sermon. She found it especially helpful to not stare down at her notes and ignore the audience but rather engage them and feed off their reactions to her words. The words sounded much more genuine when she spoke freely, less rehearsed and robotic.

Alexandra looked up and smiled at her members, receiving the same warmth back at her from everyone. The eyes of the large, silent crowd weighed on her as she also sensed the eyes of Jesus Christ peering down at her from behind, built into the gorgeous stained-glass mural above the altar.

"Good morning," she began, questioning her topic once again. "I'd, uh, like to take today to discuss David."

Some members nodded their heads, willing to hear her take on such an important biblical figure.

"Now we've all heard about David. He beat the mighty giant, Goliath, and became king of Israel. He has more writings about him than anyone else in the Bible."

Even muttering the name *David* brought back a deep sadness for the loss of her friend. After so many years, she missed him as much now as the day he was taken from her. She drew a quick breath to remember David, and her eyes filled. She pushed down the feelings, strangling the emotion so it didn't overtake her in public. There would be time for that later. She needed to be there for the crowd now. Her dedication, while noble, was also to her own detriment.

"David was the youngest son of Jesse, the Bethlehemite. He was ruddy, with beautiful eyes and a handsome appearance." The description made her remember David's penetrating green eyes. "Sounds like my kind of guy," she joked, a single tear falling down onto her sermon notes, landing where *David* was written out.

She sniffled quietly and proceeded. "He spent his time tending to his father's sheep. He was somewhat isolated, dealing with seasonal weather extremes and dangerous predators and fending for himself. But through all that, he kept his faith strong and prayed quite a bit. He didn't realize all his menial labor was not unlike other significant biblical figures. Servants and leaders of God often came from obscurity. They were unapplauded and unappreciated, never getting the chance to take a break for their own well-being. No one notices someone like this, except God. God 'looks at man's heart and not his appearance. He sees not as man does.' God sees each person for who they are meant to be."

Alex started to find her flow with the sermon and tried to get past her last-minute worries on the subject.

"Now David's hard work, for all those years, was just training. His father trusted him all that time with his flock, as he understood his son's integrity and level of responsibility. At this same time, Israel was in a bad way. They had a king who was never seen and was failing them. This caused the people of Israel to move away from God, feeling he was also an absentee king who had seemingly forgotten about them. Now God spoke with a messenger named Samuel, who was told to find a new king for Israel. And God led him to Jesse's land, where he met David and was sent divine word to elect this young man. David outright laughed at the notion but was soon anointed in front of his brothers by Samuel and given the path to find his full potential, as crazy as it may have seemed. But David was ready for the task, even if he didn't think so at first. Now, as I mentioned earlier, this is the same David who killed Goliath, with no fear of such a beast thanks to years of protecting his father's flock from predators. He stood his ground and defeated the giant with a very unorthodox means."

Alex stopped quickly, the last few sentences reminding her of how her David saved her from Blackheart as he threw her aside during that battle. David caught her and then took that hard hit from the beast, shielding her. As she tried to refocus, she found Rebecca in the crowd, who gave Alex a reassuring smile that helped her finish. She reveled in that warm, maternal feeling she wished she could remember from her own mother.

"And he was able to get beyond his fear and doubts and continued on to achieve greatness as king, heralding forty years of prosperity for Israel and bringing its people back to the Lord. God worked through David to regain the faith of his people, giving them hope and reason to believe. Now, David made few mistakes, some involving infidelity, but nonetheless, he died making a difference to many people. His memory lives on . . ."

She thought of her David again and paused, unsure of the exact message she wanted to put across. Was it to remain hopeful? Or just to reflect on her lost friend? Sermons were still not her strong point. Given her thoughts of David and the frustration she felt, she ended prematurely before she became any more vulnerable in front of the crowd. She completed the sermon, and the congregation stared blankly at her at its conclusion. She waited for any type of response to break the immense silence. They all stood and clapped loudly, praising her efforts. A deep sense of accomplishment filled her.

Minutes later, the service concluded, and the friendly crowd greeted one another to enjoy coffee and cookies. None of them used plates and just let the crumbs scatter all around the entranceway of the church. Alex noted this and realized she'd have another fun-filled afternoon of vacuuming the narthex.

She was given hugs by several members, who were all very supportive and loving.

One pulled her aside. "I'm sorry I haven't been here for a few months. We were all devastated to hear about your dad. How are you holding up?"

"Okay, I guess. As good as can be," Alex responded.

"He was a good man."

"Yes, he was."

"The holidays are going to be hard this year for you."

"Probably."

"They're going to be really, really hard," the woman said, inadvertently making Alex feel worse about the loss of her parent.

"Okay," Alex said, trying to bypass her.

An older gentleman pulled Alex aside, almost spilling her coffee. "You're doing really well up there. It takes time, but you'll get there," he said, clearly using the exchange as an introduction for another agenda. "Your dad left some big shoes to fill."

Alex started to speak but he cut her off.

"I think you and my grandson would really hit it off," he said.

"I, uh—" she stammered, looking for another exit.

"Hey, when is this week's group meeting again?" another member called out to her.

She felt overwhelmed from all the commotion around her.

Christian, Rebecca, and Adam saw her struggling. Rebecca grabbed her and gave her a big hug, cutting off everyone else. Christian and Rebecca looked slightly older than when Meadowsville was freed from Blackheart's grasp, and Christian also appeared war-torn. Teenaged Adam had shaggy hair, accompanied by baggy jeans, a polo shirt that was a size too big, and the shadow of blooming facial hair surrounding his face.

"Just focus on me, sweetie. Ignore them. They mean well. Just have weird ways of showing it," Rebecca said calmly, relieving much of Alex's anxiety.

The warm, genuine hug meant more to her that anyone could have known. There was no reason for it other than to show her love and support. Rebecca had been so good about doling out hugs since Alex had come back to town.

Christian forced a smile at Alex as Adam grabbed several cookies for himself. One of Christian's concealed knives poked him, and he adjusted it under his dress pants. He always kept at least one weapon on him at all times, even all these years later, as he was still very concerned about Blackheart returning. There was no evidence to support it, but he just had a feeling he couldn't escape from, and no one could convince him otherwise. He was as much a prisoner in his own mind as Alexandra felt in the church.

"How ya holding up?" Christian asked her.

"Not sure," Alex said, still holding onto Rebecca, who acted as a protective mother.

Members began to file out of the church, exchanging pleasantries on the sunny day. The large doors closed on the church, shutting Alexandra inside, trapping her there, and she was now faced with cleaning up the mess, not able to enjoy the nice weather. Even a tiny bit of positivity seemed so out of reach.

Rebecca offered to help her clean up. Christian walked around the church, methodically checking all of the windows, locks, and holy water levels in a specific pattern. This, much like his nightly patrols, was very routine. He had allowed his post-traumatic stress disorder to fester over the years. While his wife and son wished he would get it treated properly, he was defiant, feeling he would lose his edge and be unable to battle the monster again in such a relaxed state. Since Father Richard died, Christian and Rebecca watched over Alex, as she was all alone.

As the group tidied the church together, Adam was left by himself, eating his desserts and playing a card game on his cell phone. Between his mother working a full-time schedule and his father either at work or on patrol, he had gotten used to entertaining himself. He sometimes wondered how things would have been different if Caroline were still alive. This current dysfunction was all he'd ever known.

"Holy water needs to be refilled," Christian told Alex in a serious tone. "You have to be more careful with this stuff."

"I'll take care of it later," she responded, seeing Rebecca playfully roll her eyes as they both continued to tidy the church.

"The lock on your men's room is loose. I can tighten it for you if you want," he offered.

Alex noticed Adam being quiet and asked him how he was doing. He told her he was fine but didn't lift his eyes up to look at her. Adam was never rude to her but was a fairly typical inattentive teenager.

The group finished their tasks, and Rebecca, Christian, and Adam started to leave. They all gave her individual hugs, with Rebecca whispering gently in Alex's ear, "You did great today, sweetie."

Alex smiled and enjoyed the warmth of her stand-in mother. Christian was firm and fatherly, while Adam was passive like a little brother. She rubbed his messy hair in a playful manner, and he looked up at her in disbelief. She winked at him and he smiled, finally breaking his serious demeanor as they all left. Once again, the doors shut, and

Alex saw only a bit of the sunshine as the darkness closed in on her again. She was isolated and alone. The warmth and companionship the Reed family provided was now gone.

She looked around at the empty church and continued thinking of David. Her sermon did nothing more than make her miss him. She rushed to her office, quickly shutting the curtains overlooking the empty parking lot, and started sobbing at her desk. Her role leading such a large congregation with no guidance had left her an exhausted caregiver. Her support groups every week also saw nonmembers, too, who were equally difficult to manage. She had no outlet for her feelings, and they continued to build up inside. But so many depended on her. Should she even entertain the concept of leaving them all to find herself? Was that a terrible thought? Was she just being selfish?

Maybe having a significant other to love and support her would help. Maybe she needed someone else, but maybe she didn't. This was something else she wished her mother was still around to help her understand better. She didn't like the idea of submitting to a husband, which was how she had felt growing up under her father's tutelage, but it sure could help with big life decisions. Just having that other person to trust and rely on, having an active part in her life. She did, deep down, want to have a partner, but had no direction on how to find the right person. And David—though he had been a confused, angry, and lost teenager—had opened her eyes in a way she never thought possible. While he matched none of the criteria she felt would be suitable for her, her experience with him made her doubt everything she had assumed about men until that point.

Not that it even mattered, as her random attempts at dating all fell short. There were never any adequate prospects, so she disregarded the thoughts. Why bother thinking about any of it? No one seemed to appreciate the dedication to her trade or the lifestyle she had chosen for herself. And she didn't want to apologize for caring so deeply about such an honorable calling. David would have understood, but he wasn't here and wasn't coming back. It hurt so bad every time she grounded herself in the reality of the situation.

She continually struggled with her decision to run the church after her father died. There was a sense of obligation that made her do it, but she questioned it every day. Aside from the pressure of the church and community, and the memories of David, she was constantly reminded of Blackheart. Even with the beast gone physically, he still had a strong presence. The town would never forget the pain and destruction all those years back. Christian was a constant reminder of it with his concerning behavior and constant overbearing presence in her life.

She left her office, wiped the tears, and went out to the graveyard. She passed the graves of countless children, most of whom had been killed by either John Smith or Blackheart. She arrived at David's grave. He was the only man she ever had a meaningful connection with. Despite the circumstances surrounding their relationship, the brevity of their friendship, and his tragic, premature demise, he remained very important to her, even after all this time. What she wouldn't give for him to be back. Even just for a moment. Even if just to see his lovely green eyes once more. The same matching eyes that looked back at her every time she saw a mirror.

He was with her in spirit, and she felt him, but she wished for more. She could move on if she knew he was finally at peace. Even with all her uncertainties, she knew God would heal him of all his troubles and care for him better than anyone of this world could. She picked a small yellow flower from a tiny patch behind her and put it on his grave.

"I hope you found your peace. You're with Him now. No more pain or worry. He'll take care of you," she expressed, feeling a heavy heart again.

She wanted to believe her own words, but they didn't feel completely genuine. She was conflicted, filled with the self-centeredness of wanting him back and yet not wishing to take him away from the path God chose for him. Blind faith in God's decisions was difficult, and He seemed to want people to use Him as a crutch during the most difficult times. But after years of seemingly nothing happening, finding no apparent benefit, she became very impatient and downtrodden. No one explained how to endure. People were supposed to follow His word and trust Him no matter what.

She walked away from David's grave. She had hoped somehow to hear his sweet voice, but she left in silence, disappointed once again. She remembered the fun they had had together after her initial apprehension of her father accepting him, and she smiled as the bright sun warmed her face. It had been the last time she truly felt happy.

The light made her lips tingle, causing her think of the only kiss she'd ever received—from David. It seemed like he was looking down on her and letting her know he was okay and to trust in God. That things were bigger than she realized, but no matter how out of control everything seemed, He is always in control.

A cloud covered the sunshine, and a cool breeze ran over her. She began to walk back to her office and looked down to see John Smith's grave. She always hated knowing this memorial was on her grounds. John Smith's body had never been recovered and was assumed to be on Chrysanthemum Drive along with Blackheart. No one dared remediate the land for fear of giving new life to either of those awful creatures.

She glared at the gravestone before walking back to the church. A single crow watched her from above, following her every move with its soulless eyes.

3

Old Habits

That night at nine o'clock, Christian left the Meadowsville Market decked out in fully customized armor. He had stopped going to work when Caroline was killed, but after becoming a local legend by killing Blackheart, he was reinstated shortly after.

He looked around the rear of the store as he tightened his reinforced bulletproof upper body armor. He had several large knives hooked into his utility belt, along with a pistol loaded with silver bullets. He pulled his gloves tight, admiring the extra grips on each finger, with small tubes connected to a tiny camelback full of holy water. With the flick of his wrist, his gloves could be soaked in the evil-defying substance in seconds. He stomped at the ground to make sure his heavy-duty work boots were not loose and shimmied his legs to ensure the padding was in place around the braces on his knees. His shoelaces were paracords with ferrocerium-tipped flint fire-starter tips. He held a shiny, serrated silver ax at his side with a small prayer inscribed in it from the book of Ephesians. *I have not stopped giving thanks for you, remembering you in my prayers.* This referred to the loss of his daughter, Caroline, at the hands of David.

He looked around the streets, seeing an active yet controlled nightlife. When the sun set, there was no more fear than when it was high in the sky. There were no more curfews, roaming gangs, or restrictions for Meadowsville. Aside from normal mishaps that any other town would experience, Meadowsville had been at peace for fifteen long years. But he didn't trust it would continue. Why would he risk not being totally prepared if, God forbid, Blackheart came back? Or Mr. Smith? Or both?

With former Chief Jones no longer in power, the police had been proactive and were now actually enforcing all the laws, not just the ones they were directed to during Blackheart's reign all those years ago. The newer officers never saw the way things used to be. They knew only how things currently were, while the more senior officers still struggled with so many drastic transitions over the last few decades. But now with fewer citizens and businesses, and almost no tourists coming in, the community was quieter than ever. The police spent most of their tours just patrolling, trying to find things to do in order to justify their jobs on the force. On the plus side, one could safely walk the streets at anytime of night or day and get to their destination without issue.

Christian continued to patrol, blending in with the shadows, as his outfit was almost all black. There were many empty businesses and houses throughout his path. He thought back to growing up in town and seeing a bustling community. Even with the plague of Mr. Smith, Meadowsville had been a great place to live.

Several cars passed by him and beeped their horns, waving at him out of respect for their community's hero. They didn't want to, but most felt either obliged to do so or sorry for him. Christian nodded in response, not taking his attention off of his surroundings, but then heard someone yelling behind him. He turned and found two high school students laughing at him as they drove past.

"Nice outfit, faggot! We don't need you anymore! Go home, you fuckin' wacko," one yelled as the other tossed an empty soda can at his feet.

Christian watched them pass, with the amplified muffler hurting his ears, and continued on, ignoring the taunts. There were detractors in town, including the police, who were concerned he was trying to uphold a solitary vigilante mindset. But, due to his popularity, they allowed him to continue his nightly routine, hoping he remained peaceful and quiet so they didn't have to intervene.

Experiencing what had happened all those years ago and seeing the power from the villainous creature he'd battled, Christian believed a return was not a question of if but when. And he alone would be ready for it. He would be the only one who could stop it.

"You little assholes woulda been raped and killed fifty times over if it weren't for me," he said to himself, referencing Smith and Blackheart's victim patterns.

Underneath an overpass, he saw the remnants of spray paint that had been cleaned off, honoring Smith as an idol. He shook his head, disgusted at his hometown's fascination with a person like that.

He walked up Chrysanthemum Drive to view the debris of Blackheart's home. It appeared the same as it had the night before, and the one before that—ever since that giant inferno his fellow citizens created had been extinguished all those years ago. Blackheart's body had never been found. It had appeared to absorb into the earth under the house, which seemed to be a fitting end for the creature. He was buried along with his mentor, Mr. Smith, and they would both, hopefully, stay there forever. Christian gently nudged parts of the rotten and burned wood, hoping something would happen, but it didn't. He felt bit of disappointment and continued on his path.

Christian swung his ax gently as he walked down the long winding path toward the graveyard where Caroline was buried. There was no wind or movement as he veered away from the main roads, approaching Meadowsville Community Church. A small beam of moonlight shined down and illuminated Caroline's tombstone. As he got closer, he saw a small toy he brought for her birthday several weeks ago. Much like Blackheart's home, he visited Caroline every night too.

He sat on the ground in front of her grave, placing the ax beside him. He grunted, working past the pain in his hips that ailed him every day. He then retrieved a flask and drank a mouthful of straight whiskey. He breathed out, coughing at the strength of the beverage, smelling the alcohol odor of his body.

"Hey, sweetie," he said, sniffling, fighting back tears.

He looked across at the church and saw the lights turn out as Alexandra closed it up for the night and went to her small parsonage next door. She didn't notice Christian and slowly walked alone, looking defeated after the emotional day.

"Poor kid," Christian said, seeing the strife in his friend. "Hang in there, Alexandra."

He turned his attention back to Caroline.

"You should see your brother. Can you believe he's a freshman in high school now? He's so smart. And he's strong. I try to wrestle him, but he puts me down every time," he said, giggling. "I'm just an old, broken-down wannabe nowadays. I'm glad you never had to see me like this." He shifted into himself a bit more deeply.

He sat in silence briefly, thinking of hugging her before she went to sleep one night, her beautiful curly red hair spread across the messy bed as she grabbed her favorite stuffed rabbit.

"God, I miss you so much. I'd do anything to see you again," he said, now crying. "Adam, your mom . . . we all miss you every goddamned day."

Christian punched a nearby gravestone in anger, not feeling it due to the metal-reinforced knuckles in his gloves.

He still felt responsible for allowing her to die. Even with therapy, he was unable to forgive himself. His antidepressants rattled in his pocket, and he realized he had forgotten to take his medications. He pulled out three types and drank them down with his whiskey.

"This stuff is bad for you," he joked to Caroline but quickly became regretful again. "I know your mom and the doctors want me to take these things, but they don't help at all."

He stood up and nervously looked around, hearing some leaves rustle. His only company was his deep depression. He kissed his daughter's grave.

"Behave yourself. I'll see you tomorrow," he said, caressing the top of it before stumbling home, somewhat inebriated.

At home, he hung up his gear in a premade rack, brushing a small amount of dust off the shirt. He went upstairs and saw Adam lying in bed reading a book.

"Whatcha got there, buddy boy?"

"Something for school. Not very interesting," Adam replied sullenly.

"Yeah, you look thrilled," Christian joked, making them both smile. "You wanna take a break and I'll tell you a story that's much more fun? Or we can practice some self-defense drills again."

Adam put the book down and looked at his father. "No, I'm good on wrestling. But the story sounds fine," he said, humoring his father, knowing it'd be about Blackheart again.

Christian sat on his bed, and the strong odor of alcohol made Adam wince. It was well-documented that his father drank secretly, but Adam just ignored it and gave Christian his attention. Christian made it a goal to never lie to Adam about anything, as his guilt from Caroline had made him this way. The drinking, however, was something he was very ashamed of.

"So, the creature. This Blackheart. The pure, black heart . . . soul . . . and core of this town, he's bleeding all over the place. Screeching like a dying hyena. His house is burning down around him, the townspeople rioting outside. And I strike him over and over again," he said, before jumping to his feet and becoming more excited.

Rebecca walked by, hearing the interaction, and wanted to stop it but was just happy to see her husband and son bonding. Christian spent so much of his time patrolling, working, and then doing upkeep on his armor and weapons. They seemed to get whatever was left of him after all those things took priority. She went into her bedroom to ready herself for the night.

Adam sat at attention, humoring Christian, even though he knew the story already. He loved his father, but his lifestyle habits had become a bit much.

"The creature strikes back and knocks me around, but I keep getting back up and battling. Showing it I was not afraid. I was going to beat him that night no matter what. And I stabbed him with a flaming piece of wood, delivering the death blow . . ."

Christian then realized that by previously disregarding his family, he had allowed them to be easily accessible to Blackheart. And he lost Caroline because of it. When Blackheart held Adam as a baby, it was the most horrific thing Christian ever encountered, next to seeing Caroline's dead body. He never told his son he was once in that dangerous situation. He suddenly became conflicted—his nightly patrols were the same habitual activity as before but he justified them more. He stopped his story and patted Adam's foot, now totally unsure of himself.

"Part two some other time."

"Good stuff, Pop," Adam said sarcastically.

Christian went to leave the room and then asked Adam how school was going. Adam replied it was as exciting as hearing about Blackheart for the ten-thousandth time, zinging his father, who enjoyed the friendly banter. Christian smiled as they bid each other good night, and he entered his room with Rebecca. Adam let out a sigh of relief and shook his head in disbelief at his father's behavior.

Christian remembered he forgot to chew gum when he came in and saw Rebecca's concerned face as she, too, smelled the alcohol on him.

"How is she?" she asked about Caroline, knowing Christian's nighttime ritual.

Christian put his medications on the nightstand and started crying again. He put his head into his hands and leaned over. Rebecca hugged him hard, and they reminisced about their lost daughter. She didn't bring up the drinking but had noticed over the past few months that it was getting worse. She was afraid of hurting Christian by bringing it up, but it was an inevitable conversation. They comforted each other for a while before going to bed. Christian lay awake most of the night, anxious about his patrolling the following day.

4

Support Group

The next day, Alexandra led her weekly support group. She had developed these when she returned to town for the remaining members of the community who still needed help processing the events of Smith and Blackheart's reign of terror. They requested the meetings, and she was happy to oblige them, being the only church in town willing to do so. Thirty of its normal attendees sat around the special event room of the church, discussing their own personal tragedies stemming from Blackheart. It was a somber yet supportive group. The room was a basic, white-walled, gray-tiled area that offered little to no auditory or visual stimulation. It was perfect to keep the members focused on the group itself.

"He took my son. He went missing for almost an entire year, and then we get the call that his body was found. He was just left mangled a few blocks away. Just left in a creek like a piece of trash," one older man put out to everyone, who all displayed remorse for him. "And whenever I called the police, they blew me off. Said they were doing everything under their power to find out what happened, which was an outright lie. My son is dead. Never coming back. And who knows how many other people felt that same pain. That Mayor Wilkins should burn in hell."

Alex was startled at the man's last comment as he raised his voice in anger. The group seemed to nod in agreement at the statement, which was very unlike them. Alex wanted them all to feel like this was a safe zone to express themselves, but she was not a qualified mental health professional, so she was unable to find the right way to manage their—at times—extreme feelings.

If you were better at your job, you'd be better able to be support them, the negative voice fired off in Alex's mind. She shook off the thought and returned her attention to the attendees.

"They used to be so terrible. Thank God that's changed. My nephew is on the force, and the entire department is different now," a middle-aged woman put out. "Not taking away from your loss, which I'm so sorry to hear. Like my daughter. She just got married, and a month after the wedding, she and my son-in-law were left in pieces in their new house."

The group all nodded and continued listening empathetically to one another. The hostility seemed to be more intense and was elevating rapidly.

"All these tragedies have brought us together," Alex interjected uncomfortably. "Together we are stronger, and under Him, we are unbeatable. We all lost loved ones—"

"Not me," another middle-aged man cut in. "I didn't lose anybody . . . just my livelihood. I worked at the post office for twelve years. They downsized because of everyone leaving town, and I've been working like a dog for minimum wage ever since. And there's no other jobs out there either. I don't think I've made my bills for a given month in a decade. I am in a painful amount of debt. I can't even afford to leave."

"Me too," another woman added. "My husband was making six figures as the township clerk. With no one left to pay taxes, they cut his pay in half. And the benefits ate up the rest. We struggled for years before he finally left. I had to stay here for my mom, who's older and needs help every day. But he didn't care. He cut and ran."

"And you got the damned lunatic running around like a superhero, fighting shadows. Someone should stick him in a padded room and throw away the key," another member added.

Alex was taken aback by the unusual topics being raised by the normally subdued attendees and swallowed hard at the rising volatility. While she wanted to defend Christian, he did make it much harder for the town to move on—and made her job harder.

"Almost makes you wish for the good ol' days to come back. At least we were able to live more comfortably. Even with that thing running around . . . Blackheart . . . whatever it was. The pros greatly outweighed the cons to being here," another man said.

Alex had a visceral reaction to that statement and was unable to keep her feelings restrained. She'd reached the pinnacle of her patience. Alexandra felt the aggravation building to this and didn't like the emotional connection as it related to Blackheart. That monster did not deserve their energy.

"Okay, stop," she blurted out, catching the attention of the entire group. "I understand things are frustrating right now. For all of us. The loss of friends, family, financial support. Loss is always a hard thing to endure."

She remembered David smiling at her, and she became much more emotional. She choked on her words briefly but regained her composure. The group watched Alex sympathetically, feeling the sincerity of her words.

"I also lost someone very close to me. And it's awful and terrible, and I'd do anything to bring them back. But I try to remain steadfast with my beliefs in His power. God is there for us during these hard times. Our faith should not be made or broken during hardships but rather reaffirmed and strengthened. Events like that are the closest to hell we will ever have to experience. So we understand how dreadful it is. We can one day ascend and fully appreciate the Lord and His kingdom of heaven in all its glory."

She paused, much like in her sermons, not sure how to put together a fitting conclusion, but she was now too exasperated to think clearly. "We have all the tools to aid us in our recoveries, whether doctors, medications, our faith, or each other. He has given us everything we need. Wishing for an evil like that to descend upon us again would be doing a great injustice to what we've worked so hard to achieve these past few years. And it would do nothing but bring us back down to that dark place we knew so well. We would bring about our own demise. It would be hell on earth. We should be striving for something more. And I believe this town can do better. We have to."

Each of the members looked toward the floor or outside at the trees, staying silent in reflection of their mindsets and words during the meeting. She looked around at the puzzled faces of her attendees.

"Time's up," she said, seeing that the hour-long meeting was now over.

Everyone thanked her and left the church. Alex once again watched the large doors close and realized this was the first time she had heard someone other than Christian utter the name *Blackheart* in many years. Even the mention of him sent a cold shiver down her spine. She recalled his evil face leering over her inside the church when she had had the unpleasant experience of making his acquaintance.

5

Self-Sufficient

Adam stood in front of his dirty gym locker. The locker room showed paint peeling off the walls, a floor with deteriorated cement, and lockers dented in so badly they were hard to open. The stench of body odor and urine flooded the air.

He dreaded another day of running the track. *Nothing like the gratifying sensation of sweating outside and then going back to class to sit there for another two hours, stinking like an old shoe,* he thought.

Adam was the last one in the locker room, delaying his attendance in class, but saw the clock and realized he'd be late. As he took off his pants and slid on his favorite red basketball shorts, he heard someone talking to him.

"Hey, Adam. Where's the vampires? Or was it werewolves? Where's your daddy to save us?" someone called from around the other side of the lockers.

Bruce, who was an eleventh grader and Adam's constant antagonist, targeted his father each and every time. Unbeknownst to Bruce, Adam trained with Christian a few nights each week, working on submission holds and striking techniques. Christian always made it clear to Adam that fighting should be the last resort but to always be ready to defend himself. The only times he and Christian had been able to bond was when it dealt with Blackheart in some way—war stories, self-defense, and even occasionally Adam helping Christian clean his weapons.

Adam just wanted to have a good relationship with his parents. Even if his dad was a little strange, Adam loved him all the same. But he did feel a great deal of anger at his family's situation. As if it weren't bad enough that Caroline was gone, his mother was overworked and his father was a walking calamity.

There was one thing his parents never taught him—how to manage his feelings appropriately. And someone like Bruce badmouthing his parents, knowing how much they worked and all their hardships, infuriated Adam.

Bruce walked around the lockers to come within a few feet of Adam. Another boy Adam didn't know joined them.

"'Sup, faggot?" Bruce said.

"Hey, Bruce. How are you today?" Adam responded sarcastically.

"What'd you say?"

Adam repeated himself, acting as if he spoke to a disabled person, using sign language and modified speech in a joking way.

"You think you're funny?"

"I don't think I'm not funny," Adam teased back.

Adam stepped over the built-in bench behind him to walk past, but Bruce followed, continuing to block him.

"You got some mouth on you. Surprising, because you have such an asshole father. Figure you'd just keep to yourself. Spare any further embarrassment," Bruce said, becoming more physically confrontational.

Adam politely asked him to move, trying to withhold his anger, but Bruce and his friend just stood there. As Adam tried to push past, Bruce slammed Adam's locker shut and shoved him hard, causing him to lose his footing. Adam had hoped it wouldn't come to this, but he now had no choice. He stood up and collected himself as the two aggressors laughed. Normally, their interactions ended without coming to blows, but today seemed to be different. Adam didn't want to fight the boys, but it seemed he had no choice now. He had a feeling his father would understand what he was about to do.

"Yeah, real funny, guys. And you're right . . . my dad may be an asshole . . . but he taught me how to fight," he said, whipping his locker open right into Bruce's head, knocking him down.

The other boy grabbed Adam and tried to punch him, but Adam dodged, causing the boy to fracture his hand against the lockers behind him. Adam twisted his opponent's injured hand and dropped him to the ground. Bruce stood up, unable to see from a now open wound bleeding down into his eyes.

Adam pulled his locker door off and slammed it into Bruce's head again, knocking him down for good. A steady trail of blood dripped onto the floor. Bruce tried to roll over but couldn't manage.

As the other boy moved to get up, Adam stomped down on his hand. The boy screamed, and the gym teacher, Mr. Benjamin, heard the commotion all the way inside the gymnasium. He quickly ran to the locker room, his whistle dangling around his neck, to see Bruce laid out, bleeding, and Adam with the other boy in a vicious wrist lock, refusing to let go.

"What the hell are you doing?" he yelled at Adam, trying to pull him off. "Let go now!"

Several of the students were now in the locker room, watching the chaotic scene. Adam realized he'd gone too far and let go of the submission hold. He was quickly snatched up by the teacher and dragged across the school toward the principal's office. He had previously informed several teachers over the last year of Bruce's animosity toward him, but nothing was ever done. Mr. Benjamin was one of those passive teachers who refused to intervene.

"They made me do it. I told you this would happen," Adam responded, trying to strangle his laughter. "They should've brought two more to the party. Might've stood a chance."

With no other students present, Mr. Benjamin pushed Adam against a wall. "Listen to me. This ain't funny, you little asshole. I know your dad gets you a lot of leeway with things. But this is gonna be the last of it. I don't want you in my class anymore. Between all the near fights with my other students and your nasty little mouth always running behind my back, I'm done with it all. You're out."

Adam tried to act hurt by this decree but would be much more satisfied sitting in a study hall instead of gym class. So his faked seriousness turned into a smirk, further angering Mr. Benjamin.

The school nurse ran toward the injured students, making Benjamin release his grip on Adam. They looked at each other as Adam fixed his T-shirt and tried to hide his smile.

"Let's go," Benjamin said, pushing Adam toward the main office again.

Adam walked in, and all of the secretaries and guidance counselors barely looked up at him. He was a frequent visitor to the principal's office, and this was his worst offense to date. Adam strode proudly, knowing nothing would happen to him here, just like all the other times.

6

Respect Tradition

The three members of the Meadowsville planning board, Jenny, Jordan, and Juliet, sat in a small, informal meeting at town hall to discuss the town's upcoming 125th anniversary celebration. There were multiple coffee cups sitting around and an empty pizza box at the end of the oblong table.

They confirmed several food vendors, a fireworks display, a local rock band, and the current mayor, Chazz Wiggins, to go over a brief review of the town's history. With only a few weeks to spare, they needed to tie up any remaining loose ends.

"So, with the history, how are we gonna do that?" Jenny, a much younger and newer resident, asked her colleagues. "Mayor Wiggins is going to go up there and do his shtick. Do we bring up the monster stuff? Do we want to mention Mr. Smith?"

"Not a monster. At least not that we know of. Just a serial killer. The rest was just made up," said Juliet, a lifelong local.

"Well, it was a big chunk of the town's history. We probably should include it. But, then again, a lot of people don't like to talk about it," added Jordan, also a lifelong resident. "Like, look at terror attacks and natural disasters. It's not glorified or made light of. They just pay respect to what happened."

The three sat, considering the concept.

Jenny was the first to break the silence. "There was that poem all the kids used to say, right?"

"Yes. I remember because we said it religiously every night," Juliet cut in.

"Me too," Jordan agreed. "Makes me queasy thinking about it."

"So maybe just have a moment of silence for everyone lost during the tenure of Mr. Smith, everyone recites the poem, and we move on. We could do it right before the Dead Heads play. Kind of end it and go right into a crowd-friendly act," Jenny concluded.

Jenny had moved to Meadowsille only recently, as it was the one place where she could afford a house on a budding realtor's salary. Every other area around was much more expensive, whereas Meadowsville's prices had dropped dramatically over the past decade due to its crumbling economy. She would never fully understand, not having grown up in the town's troubled past, the emotions Jordan and Juliet displayed. Unknowingly, she was reintroducing the past mindset of the town, which was what had led to its massive prior problems.

Juliet and Jordan looked at one another, neither having known or personally experienced any losses from Blackheart or Mr. Smith, and agreed. Jenny felt a sense of pride as she single-handedly overruled two lifelong locals.

"And what about Christian? He killed him. We should definitely acknowledge him at some point," Jordan added.

"Yeah, but—no offense—I haven't lived here as long as you guys, but it seems like everyone is kind of tired of his little act. Don't get me wrong. He did an amazing thing for the town, but that was over a decade ago. It's not wartime anymore, but he's stuck in it. More than halfway to being a laughingstock nowadays. I'd just mention his name and leave it alone. Don't harp on it, or you're gonna see a lot of sour faces in the crowd," Jenny recommended. "We want this event to really be something special."

The three agreed and continued planning the event, having no idea just how significant the anniversary celebration would turn out to be.

7

The Darkness

Alexandra lay in bed, fast asleep, but found herself in the middle of a nightmare.

It was a bright, sunny day, and the town looked pristine. There were no empty buildings, and everything appeared to be updated. No lawn on any property was overgrown or burned. Each and every car was perfectly parked and freshly waxed. The streets were paved and clean. However, there were no people anywhere in town, as if they had all evacuated this perfect place.

The sunshine started to fade, like an eclipse. The sun began to melt, drowning out the brightness, creating a shadow that enveloped the town bit by bit. An uncomfortable darkness took over. Nothing could be seen in it, and it devoured the town with great ease. The sun finished its death, and as the last drop of it struck the ground, it illuminated the house on Chrysanthemum Drive. This was now the only structure seen in the dark.

Blackheart's mansion was fully rebuilt, and the property looked freshly manicured. It was a truly magnificent sight. The front door was wide open, slightly shifting in the breeze. The soil looked like it was alive as it moved around fluidly.

Alex then heard the voices of her father and Blackheart, which took her back to the first time she had encountered Blackheart. "You don't intimidate me, and you won't hurt me. God will protect us, and He is stronger than you could ever hope to be," Father Richard said.

"We'll see about that," Blackheart said. "And who says I'd hurt you, Father . . . when I have much better options."

In a deviation from the actual occurrence, Blackheart then turned and locked eyes with her. She recalled his piercing blue eyes, which now matched her own green hue. Then David's face appeared on Blackheart's monstrous frame, and Alexandra screamed at the hideous sight.

Alexandra jumped awake to her alarm clock radio going off. A somber song played as she sat in place, collecting herself.

I still don't know what holds me here
My entire life, I've felt like something is missing inside
Waiting and watching over me
You're the only one who understands my loneliness
I know you're there
I feel you here

She quickly turned it off and looked at the big open space next to her in bed. What she wouldn't give to have someone there just to comfort her in a moment like this. Even though it was nothing but a nightmare, it would be nice to have emotional support. She got up and walked around her quiet house. No noise, other than whatever she made herself. Everything was cleaned and in order. Breakfast for one, lunch for one, dinner for one . . . and a bed for one too. Although a tiny home, it seemed so big when it was all just for one person. She didn't spend much time in the parsonage, as it only worsened her loneliness.

Alexandra readied herself for her morning jog and didn't even bother locking the door. There was nothing of value inside the parsonage besides some pictures of her parents. She walked down the driveway and then started into a light jog as she reached the street.

Several community members waved, and she responded in kind. She wanted to stop to greet them but was afraid they would use the nice gesture as a chance to unload their problems on her. After the nightmare, she was not in the right state of mind for it.

She passed Zinnia Lane and then Red Poppy Drive. She tried to focus on her breathing but was still distracted by her nightmare—then thought of Blackheart's face again, his gnarled and evil gaze leering after her. So much pain one creature caused all these people. Anger built up in her.

She now ran harder than normal, passing Marigold Avenue. Her legs ached and her breath came harder, but she continued on. This was her only outlet for her frustrations, and she knew it. She grunted at the discomfort in her body and continued pounding the pavement. Her saliva began to thicken and her hair band slid down her silky black hair.

Foxgold Lane whipped past her and, completely fatigued, she realized her feelings were displaced. Anger, frustration, and remembrance, all representative of the street names she sprinted past, mirrored her swirling emotions. She shouldn't feel anger toward Blackheart but rather sorrow. But this was easier said than done.

Alex slowed to a walk and saw Chrysanthemum Drive a few blocks away. She moved toward it, huffing in the fresh air. She hadn't been back to this place since she went to see the wreckage after David had been killed. She never got to see his body before it was buried.

She pushed herself to ascend the road. The temperature cooled from the trees surrounding the road, allowing her to now see her breath. Her body continued to cool down, and she stepped over a few small branches in her way. She reached the top of the road and looked at the opening, where the once mighty stronghold of this town's most feared figure stood.

Despite her dream, the soil here was not moving but was just patches of fresh grass intermingled with some small growths and weeds. The house was not rebuilt, and there was nothing out of place. It was just burned wreckage. Christian's footprints formed a singular path, each print not deviating even a single inch from the others. He literally followed the exact same path every night. She held back her anger toward him, because he meant well. If only he wasn't so overbearing and mean about it all.

She paced around the property, wondering what the scene with Christian and David fighting Blackheart had looked like. She then wished she could've been there, possibly helping them and saving David. She shook her head and began the long walk back to the parsonage to write this weekend's sermon.

She showered and changed clothes before going to her office inside the church. At her desk, she checked her schedule. No one due in until five o'clock, and it was currently eight in the morning. There were no community outreaches she could do right now and nothing else to do but to sit by herself and focus, highlighting the secluded life she led. She put pen to paper but again wasn't sure what to write.

8

Appreciated Aggression

That night, Rebecca, Adam, and Christian prepared dinner. She cleaned up the stove while they put the silverware and plates on the table, then they all sat and readied themselves to eat. Rebecca made delicious breaded pork chops every Wednesday, much to her son and husband's delight.

This was the one night each week Christian would come home from work to be with his family before going on his nighttime patrol. It was very hard for him, but he forced himself to do it, especially for Alexandra. She needed him to be there for her when she visited them for dinner each week. Part of him resented her for taking him off his normal daily schedule, but he made the effort for her. He believed she needed a strong male role model in her life. It was for her own good. He didn't want to be too relaxed and let anything happen to her, like with Caroline.

Christian and Rebecca ate, looking at one another to see who would ask Adam about his issue the other day in school.

"Hey, bud, we still have to talk about what happened the other day," Christian said.

"Yeah, I know," Adam said, uninterested. "Not a big deal."

"Sweetie, we're not mad. We're just concerned. You really hurt those boys," Rebecca added. "I know you and your dad play around, but you can't use that stuff unless you're in real danger."

"I did everything I could to avoid it," Adam responded, beginning to shovel his dinner in his mouth quickly. "I even told the teachers he was bullying me. They didn't do anything."

"Slow down. Don't choke," Christian said. "Your mom and I just don't want you getting into any more trouble. You've already had a few incidents at school this year."

"Okay, maybe the other stuff I could've avoided, but this one was not like that."

Christian stayed quiet, and Adam became resentful his dad hadn't come to his defense.

"Well, they're usually making fun of you," Adam tossed at his father.

"For what?" both Christian and Rebecca asked simultaneously, totally surprised.

Adam saw a picture in his mind of Christian suited up and decided not to engage this conversation much further. He shook his head. Neither of his parents understood how the town viewed them at this point, so his words would just fall on deaf ears. "Never mind," he conceded.

"Well, Principal Gutierrez called me this afternoon. Neither boy will say it was you who hurt him, but your gym teacher witnessed it," Rebecca told them both.

"Probably because they're ashamed a freshman pounded out two seniors," Adam bragged, pretending to drop an invisible microphone.

"They're not letting Mr. Benjamin kick you out of his gym class either," Rebecca added.

"But . . . why? He said I was out." Adam snapped out of his braggadocio ways.

"Just be careful. As much as those boys probably deserved it, try to not hurt anyone at school. Or you'll end up all old and angry like your dad," Christian said, winking at Adam, showing respect for his son's actions.

Adam smiled back, looking down at his dinner.

A dog barked outside. Christian started at the sound, having a brief flashback of one of Blackheart's hounds snapping its fangs in his face. A bead of sweat fell down his left cheek.

"Hey, where's Alex tonight?" Adam asked, diverting their attention. "She loves pork chop Wednesday extravaganzas."

"She's on a date," Rebecca said. "Fingers crossed for this one."

"Who's it with?" Christian asked.

"Someone's friend from church."

Christian and Adam looked at each other playfully, making ugly faces.

"Sounds just thrilling. I know. She's trying. You gotta give her a lot of credit for that." Rebecca joined their chuckling.

"Dad, how many girls did you date before Mom?"

Christian thought hard. "I can't remember. A few."

"Me," Rebecca hopped in.

"Just you?"

"Just me. Your father knew he wouldn't get any better than me," she said, winking at Christian.

"And your mother was ruined for all other men after being with me," he pawed back, smiling.

Adam rolled his eyes at the playful and affectionate banter between his parents, but he enjoyed their brief moments of family time like this. He just wished they happened more often.

Christian nervously looked at the rustic clock on the wall over Rebecca's head, ensuring he had time to finish his meal before his nightly patrol.

9

Different Interests

Alexandra sat across from Mitchel. He was the best friend of a younger congregation member and had goaded her into accepting his invitation to be set up. Rebecca had always advised her to show something, but not everything, on a date, which made her chuckle. Alex had settled on a somewhat form-fitting dark blue sweater and a pair of jeans.

The pair sat in a trendy, stylized pizza parlor that had been in Meadowsville for only the past year called Pizza Heaven. This was agreed upon as a low-stress and informal date location. So far, it had gone well, but Alexandra remained pessimistic about the chances of it turning into anything beyond a first date. She didn't fully understand that no one would be able to compare to David, who had been a breath of fresh air in her otherwise mundane life.

But she unconsciously compared each person to him, time and time again.

"So, Mitch—"

"Mitchel, please," he corrected her.

"Okay, Mitchel," she continued despite his interruption. "What do you do for fun?"

"Great question . . . I love to ski, hike, and travel," he said, a bit cockier than she would like.

"Oh, travel? Any places you'd like to go?" she asked, having no knowledge of any of those things.

"Philippines would be a blast. South Africa. I don't know about anywhere else."

They sat in silence waiting for their food.

"So this place seems nice," Alex said.

"Yeah, seems like they got a good selection. Can't go wrong with pizza," he replied, looking around at anything but Alex.

"Nope," she put out, hoping for a bit of help carrying the conversation.

Mitchel seemed like he wanted to ask her something but was hesitant to do so. He moved in his chair uncomfortably and opened his mouth to speak but stopped himself. Luckily, their food arrived, and both sat facing personal, handcrafted pies. Alex had a plain and Mitchel had an assortment of meats and vegetables on his. She saw his food choice, much like his personality, as being much more open-minded than most of her other dates. Due to her career, she was usually set up with very routine and reserved individuals. So maybe she sold Mitchel wrong. Maybe this was the type of date she needed.

"So you're a pastor," Mitchel finally got the courage to say.

"Yeah, well, kind of. But only recently. I run a nondenominational church for the community. My dad was a priest in the Catholic Church but left to get married and start a family. It just seemed like the best path for me to take, ya know?"

"Yeah, makes sense," he replied, taking a large bite of his pizza. "So you guys can be female now? And date?"

"Yeah, when you're nondenominational, you have those types of freedoms," she said, smiling, wondering if the brief odd look on Mitchel's face was from the food being too hot or him not knowing what *nondenominational* meant. His question turned her off of the entire topic, but she continued on with it. It was the seemingly sarcastic undertone of it that she didn't appreciate, although she wasn't sure whether she was now just looking for any reason to not like this person.

"So that seems like an interesting job," he said, unsure of himself.

"It's very rewarding. You get the chance to help a lot of people," she replied passively.

"You don't seem too enthused by it," he asked.

"It's not that. It just gets a bit much at times. Like, you don't get breaks. Kind of like a constant twenty-four-seven job," she replied, realizing she'd veered the conversation into a negative space.

"Do your parents help you at all? I don't know what I'd do without mine," he said, trying to salvage the discussion.

"No, unfortunately neither one of them is around. Both passed away," she replied, unhappy with her now continued pessimism. "I'm sorry. I don't mean to sound so negative."

"No, it's fine," he said, becoming a tad more awkward. "I just have never known a priest before. I don't want to speak in any way that's offensive or anything."

Alexandra was very turned off by his comment, whether he knew it was rude or not. And by calling her a priest, he clearly wasn't listening to her. David had never been rude to her, not even once. He was too timid, which had its charm, and would never be this arrogant.

"Just be yourself. I promise I won't toss holy water on you or anything," she said, trying to be funny, but Mitchel smiled and tried to eat quicker than normal.

Alex looked down at her untouched meal and appreciated the path Mitchel took, which was the same way it always happened. As soon as she tried to talk about herself and be honest about her career being her entire life, the interest and appeal were somehow lost. It was clear to her even someone like this couldn't appreciate her choices, so what hope was left for her to meet someone who understood her situation?

"So do you do anything besides work then?" he tried to continue on, grasping at straws.

"No. That's about it, Mitchel," she said, watching him feign interest in her.

Alexandra signaled for the waiter and asked for her food to be packed up. "Mitchel, you seem like a nice guy. I'll just make this easy for you," she said grabbing her meal and putting fifteen dollars on the table to cover her expenses. "This just isn't working, is it?"

Mitchel, being genuine for the first time, agreed with her, shaking his head. Alex thanked him for the company, blessed him in a very sarcastic way to amuse herself, and left the restaurant. She got to her car and slumped back in the seat, tossing her food aside. She yelled in frustration and convinced herself it was her own fault for the date not going well. *Was it what I wore? Why can't I stop being so negative? What will the congregation think of me with this setup not going well?*

The thoughts race through her mind as she started the car and the radio automatically came on. A female vocalist sang deeply and calmly, with an electric guitar in the background.

I thought I had everything, but look at me
Wish I could have a wicked mind or a body for sin
Just take me and soak it in
I'll show you why I'm worth it
But I'll never be quite enough
I just wanna die

She sat quietly and heard the timely lyrics. She now understood what David had told her about loneliness during the time they spent together. It was always there and was completely dependable. Her phone rang and it was Rebecca.

"Hello, Alex?"

"Hey, Mom."

"We all hope your date went well. We missed you at pork-chop night tonight. I made extra and can bring it over to you tomorrow after work."

"Aw . . . you're the best," Alex said in a shaky voice.

"You okay? How did it go? Seems kind of early to be over?"

"Yeah, no such luck. He just didn't understand. Feel like I was too negative, but I don't really know. I'm getting tired of thinking about it so much."

"I'm sure you did okay. This is just a bad patch."

"Seems like it's long shot to have all this bad luck. Maybe it's just me. Maybe I'm meant to be alone."

"Oh, honey, don't be crazy. You're gorgeous, fun, and have a lot to offer. And one day, you'll find someone who sees those same qualities I do."

"I already did," Alex muttered to herself, thinking of David.

"What?"

"Nothing," Alex dismissed Rebecca. "I'd even settle for just some friends at this point."

"You have friends. Look at everyone at the church, right?"

"No, unfortunately, they're just friendly to me when they need something or wanna compare me to my dad or tell me what I need to do differently for myself. I know it sounds weird, but it's true. They act like I don't know what's best for me. Does that make sense, or do I sound crazy?"

"No, I get it. That's very challenging."

"But that's my job. And it keeps me busy nonstop. No time to do anything else. And that's why I get paid to do this. I just have to keep my faith and push through, right?"

"Well, we love you for you. And we're here anytime day or night, if you need us. You're so much stronger than you realize. You should know that."

Alex stopped at a red light and realized it was where Blackheart had torn her door off and kidnapped her. She breathed heavily and tried to control her body, quickly driving through it when the light turned green. She ended her conversation with Rebecca and drove up to her pitch-black parsonage. Once again, she'd spend the night alone.

She walked upstairs into her bedroom and sat on the bed, not bothering to turn on any lights. She saw her polished wood memory box sitting on the nightstand on her side of the bed. The moonlight illuminated it just enough to shine. She opened it up and saw a picture of her mother. She had flowing brown hair, soft features, and a smile that could bring light to the darkest place imaginable.

"God, I wish you were here. I need help only you could've given me. There's so much I don't know."

She took a deep breath, releasing it into a sigh. She then saw a picture of her with her father and wished the same for him too. She desperately needed someone to help her find herself and give clarity. She kept her faith that God would fill that role, but she struggled, waiting for Him to take action.

"What else do I have to learn? What else do I need to do?" she called out to Him.

After waiting for a response and feeling silly for it, she put the pictures of her parents against her heart and sighed one last time before putting them back in her box.

She lay in bed and remembered when David used to watch her from the window. It helped her feel comfortable and allowed for a good night's sleep, like there was someone always watching over her who appreciated her for who she really was. No judgment. Just understanding and empathy.

10

Positive Experience

*avid and Alexandra sat in Father Richard's office
one night, waiting for him to call them for dinner.
Alexandra thumbed through one of her father's
old textbooks about the practical applications of biblical
teachings. She was preparing to enter the clergy in the next
several years and one day would be chosen to run the church.
David pretended to read a magazine but was actually staring
at her coyly. She began to smile uncontrollably, as it was the
first time a man had appreciated her company so much. She
looked back at him as the two briefly held eye contact with
one another but didn't speak a word. Their matching green
eyes met like two sets of stars in the night sky. They both looked
down, still smiling, flattered by each other.*

Alexandra woke up gently in her room the next morning,
unaware she had fallen asleep. She slowly sat up and looked

out the window, hoping to see David's face smiling back, but it wasn't there. A bright sun-glare poured into her bedroom, but a dark cloud quickly covered it up. Disappointment filled her at the start of another day.

11

Old Times

Meadowsville police officer whose uniform tag read *Young* patrolled the suburban section of the town. The houses all showed wear and tear and looked like ruins compared to the state they were in twenty years ago. There had been no calls during the first half of his tour, and he resisted the urge to fight his boredom with a nap. No one would even have noticed if he did. Twenty years on the force and he felt like he was no better than a rent-a-cop nowadays.

He stopped by a substation building of the fire department that housed the ambulances, EMTs, and only a few firefighters. He rang the bell and was let in to use the bathroom. The firefighters were inside watching realty television and having their late-morning coffee.

"You guys have any bites today?" Officer Young asked.

"Nothing yet," one responded. "You?"

"Nope."

They sat watching the TV for a moment.

"You guys remember years ago? The gangs, Mr. Smith and his dogs, and all that?"

Most of the firefighters nodded in agreement. The others were too young to have been in the department during that time.

Officer Young poured himself a cup of coffee and nearly drank it down in one gulp.

"Kept things interesting. We never had tours like this with nothing to do. If we weren't out on calls, we were at the station writing reports on incidents. Made the time go by quick," one of firefighters responded.

"Got that right."

Officer Young used the bathroom and heard a call as he washed his hands. It was in his assigned area and involved a pair of neighbors complaining of their dogs assaulting one another. He responded that he was on the way.

All the firefighters started laughing, as did Young.

"Hey, how about I stay here and you guys take this one? You up for a couple of dogs humpin' each other?" he asked, chuckling with his fellow municipal workers before going back to his patrol car.

Having been on the force for two decades, Officer Young got very used to responding only to select calls during the early part of his career. All the advanced directives handed down from former Police Chief Jones were very different back then. The current chief, Chief Flynn, was very much by-the-book and had turned the department into a much more efficient and honest place to work. The newer officers, knowing nothing but the current regime, were comfortable with their job duties, but Young and the more senior officers were indifferent even after all the years of change.

Young drove to the houses. Upon seeing the patrol car, virtually all the neighbors came out of their homes to see what was going on. He waved to them and approached the two elderly gentlemen who are the source of the call.

"This piece of shit let his lab violate my poodle," a bald man yelled to Officer Young.

"You shoulda kept your whore poodle inside the fence line. She was askin' for it," a chubbier man called back.

Officer Young looked up at the direct sun, hoping to blind himself and go out on long-term disability. No such luck. He was going to have to deal with this.

"Guys, never mind. Did anyone get bit? Is either dog hurt?" he asked, trying to control the situation.

The old men keep yelling back and forth as Officer Young stood between them, keeping his composure in the inane situation. Two other police cars pulled up to control the forming crowd, and Young looked at the scene, wondering how everything went from one extreme to the other in Meadowsville.

12

Getting Closer

lexandra lay in bed, struggling through another nightmare, which were normally rare for her.

A hidden, mysterious figure watched the church from the darkness. It was the middle of the day, but somehow the light avoided it.

As the figure entered the church, it walked around the pews and ignited the candles with its gnarled fingertips before moving to the altar. It stepped up without hesitation and stared up at the Jesus Christ picture in the window. After a moment, it stood at the wooden podium overlooking the nave.

Surreally, Alexandra saw herself standing at the altar, looking up at this individual.

"You're as close to God as I can get," Blackheart said, reminding her of his statement and attack on her years back.

Once these words were uttered, the church crumbled, and she felt herself being crushed underneath the wreckage. The figure at the altar remained unharmed and offered her no help, as if it just needed her to accomplish its objective and then it would dispose of her.

Now, unable to move, she saw the large shadow looming over her. The sunlight beat down on her face, burning her eyes, not allowing her to see who created the large silhouette.

She jumped awake, shaken, as an upbeat song came from her radio alarm.

Standing all alone
Everything is ready
Watching in a trance
Arrival is imminent
Are you sure
Here we go . . .

Alexandra wondered why she was having so many nightmares lately, especially ones that were linked. Her congregation members had developed a negative mindset, and she wondered whether somehow Blackheart was influencing everyone from beyond the grave. Fearing the worst, she grabbed her laptop and checked whether there had been any Blackheart sightings. Part of her didn't want to know, even if he did somehow come back. But she normally never had experiences like this, so she was unnerved by them.

"How would he be getting into my dreams?" she asked herself out loud.

She'd done everything in her power to avoid the fallen legend. She was surprised to see *Blackheart* come up immediately after she typed the letters *B* and *L*. That meant there was a growing number of people thinking about him and actively searching for information.

The first search result that came up was the Meadowsville message board, built for community members to report issues with the town so the mayor could respond. Four of the top ten topics involved Blackheart, while the rest were concerns about the 125th anniversary celebration.

Alexandra opened up one thread and it read:

I miss the days when this town was making money. I want my money back! Bring back the Blackheart!

You want money over your safety?

Your face stinks.

Do I smell asshole? Leave town if you want money. We don't want you here.

I agree. This town is no fun anymore.

Eat shit. All of you. Another reason I wish he was back. So mongoloids like you would be a meal for him.

Alexandra had a bad feeling about where the town was headed. Even if this were some dumb joke by kids, Blackheart was a growing presence again. He was causing animosity and division among the people even while not being physically present. And he was engaging her specifically for some reason.

Alex grabbed her cell phone to call Christian, but she didn't want to upset him. She believed even the notion of Blackheart being back would send him into a mental health crisis. She sat with the feelings and remained anxious, unsure of what to do and having no one to counsel her. No one would believe her even if she reached out to her local colleagues.

13

Wishful Thought

Christian spent another night sitting drunkenly at Caroline's grave. He remembered the small memorial service held at the hospital after David's attack on his family. Father Richard had presided over Christian, a still badly injured Rebecca, and Adam prior to them all officially separating. Neither Christian nor his wife could stand seeing their daughter in such a desecrated form, so they opted for a small memorial service only they could attend. Adam was screaming the entire time, and both Christian and Rebecca were inconsolable too. Alexandra came with her father but, shortly after the service began, she excused herself to try to contain her emotions.

Christian took another drink from his flask, near tears, and fought his better judgment to take his prescriptions.

He began to nod off when a call from Rebecca woke him. He quickly answered it, despite having altered vision from the booze.

"Yeah, hi," he answered.

"Hey, babe. Where are you?" she asked, already aware of his location.

"I'm uh . . . still at the store . . . inventory kept me here late."

"You're a bad liar," she kidded.

They stayed quiet for a minute before she asked how he was doing. Christian started crying into the phone, feeling a mixture of remorse for lying but also for spending time away from her and Adam again.

"I don't know why I keep doing this. It's not fair to you guys."

"Honey, honey, please try to relax. I know it's hard without her. Adam and I both miss her so badly too."

"I should've been there to protect her," Christian said.

"But you would've been if you had known. It was an accident. A terrible, terrible thing that none of us could've prevented."

Christian looked around and threw his flask down in anger. "I don't know why I come here alone. I don't know why I do any of this anymore."

"Have you talked to the therapist about it?"

"No. I don't want to. I hate going there," he said, not admitting he hasn't gone to a session in many months and had gone only sporadically before then.

Rebecca appreciated his honesty but was scared for his mental state. "If it's okay, I'd like to go there and cry with you sometime," she asked politely.

"Yeah, that'd be nice," Christian said, trying to regain his balance.

"Why don't you come home and we can talk? I'd really like to see you. Can you do that for me?" she asked of her husband in the gentlest way.

"Okay, I'll be there in a bit."

They hung up and Christian began walking home, but he tripped over a low gravestone. John Smith's gravestone. He caught himself and realized what caused his mishap. He kicked with all his might, hurting his knee. He then thought back to battling Blackheart and the overwhelming high he got from it.

"I'd give anything for you to come back one more time. They'd all stop laughing at me and show me the respect I deserve," he muttered before vomiting from his intoxication. Unbeknownst to Christian, his desire for such a thing inadvertently contributed to the growing attitude of the other Meadowsville inhabitants, all hopeful Blackheart would be back at some point.

"And there isn't anything I wouldn't give to be able to hurt you one more time for what you did to my Caroline," he finished, spitting on the grave.

Christian staggered on his way home, and it took him almost two hours to get there. He sobered up quite a bit during the walk. He finally reached his house and looked at the small patch of earth where he'd seen Caroline dead—the grass never fully grew back.

He went inside, where he was greeted by both Adam and Rebecca. They gave him a group hug, which he desperately needed. Christian loved his family and understood he needed to stop his behavior before it affected them anymore.

14

Inadvertent Resurrection

On Easter Sunday, Alexandra prepared to give her longest and possibly most significant sermon yet. Her congregation was even larger than normal, and she used her performance anxiety to fuel herself. She also did her best to bypass her uneasiness about the nightmares she'd been experiencing.

"Happy Easter," she began, to the delight of everyone.

"Happy Easter to you, Alex," they all said back.

"I want to open this up to the crowd a bit today. What is the first thing that pops into your mind when you think about Easter? Don't think. Just blurt it out."

"Chocolate bunnies!"

"Jelly beans!"

"A stuffed rhinoceros."

Everyone laughed at the last comment, coming from an endearing toddler sitting with his parents.

"Wow! I guess sugar isn't an issue to this congregation," she joked.

The crowd sat, showing sincere interest in her words on this important day.

"Does anyone think of Jesus Christ?"

Everyone nodded.

"Because that's what this day is all about. Sure, we can have some fun with the candies and festivities and all, but we should still pay homage to the amazing events that went on many years ago with our savior."

Alex began to feel a little uneasy but ignored the odd sensation.

"Easter is a reminder that God breathes new life. Each and every Easter story results in realizing God's love for us. When we are in doubt, He finds a way to deepen our faith and understanding of Him. You see, on Good Friday, Jesus was crucified, died, and was buried in a tomb. Mary Magdalene wept for Him for three days straight. And on the third day, He rose from the dead. He consoled those who had lost hope and assured them the suffering we will have to endure in this life will lead us to salvation . . . to eternal life . . . to Him."

Alex now felt the sensation grow, resembling a migraine but it was more unique. She ended her sermon prematurely.

"Let us pray . . ." When everyone bowed their heads, she continued. "Lord God, thank you for sacrificing your only son for our sinful ways. We confess it all to you to renew us."

The sensation became stronger, but she tried to push past it. She felt Blackheart's presence somehow, as if he were standing in front of her. He was there with her. She was so sure of it.

"When sin and evil work against us, we remain steadfast and true to You. We trust that Your word is the only word, and You will guide us in the most righteous way. Give us Your light and give us the chance to be reflections of Your peace during a time when this world needs Your presence and healing. Help give us the strength to help those who experience hard times, pain, death, and other worldly misfortunes. Be with us as we rejoice in Your triumphs."

She felt off balance and stumbled but steadied herself on the pulpit. Several members got out of their seats to help her but stopped when she caught herself. In her mind, Alexandra saw Blackheart's mansion in its present form, and she felt his power surge.

"Whoever believes in You will be given new life," she said, now seeing Blackheart's burnt hand crash out of the debris on Chrysanthemum Drive.

The connection to him became fully established in that moment. He had penetrated her mind, sapping her strength to energize his comeback.

She crashed to the floor of the alter.

Christian sprinted to the stage and began checking her vitals. She was alive but unconscious. Christian told everyone to back away, and he carried her to the couch in her office. He was distraught over the sight of her in such a weakened state. He stayed with her as the rest of the shaken churchgoers waited to hear how she was doing. Rebecca, unsure what else to do, assured everyone Alexandra was okay and just got overheated. They all had their post-service desserts and coffee, waiting for another update from Christian.

15

Chasing Ghosts

That night, Christian suited up and went on his patrol. After the scare with Alexandra earlier, he was feeling especially anxious. Luckily, she was fine, but the sight of her collapsing triggered Christian's fear of not being able to protect her, much like with Caroline.

He walked on his normal path, passing Daffodil Drive, Daisy Way, and Lily Lane, not realizing all the street names encompassed rebirth and new life, en route to Caroline's grave, gripping his ax a little harder than normal. His hands ached, but he didn't let it stop him. He noticed the town was much quieter than normal, and there was a feeling in the air—something different he couldn't pinpoint.

He heard footsteps and looked around quickly, only to see shadows around him. The streetlights, mailboxes, and trees all created an army of assorted shadows surrounding him. He looked at them one by one, waiting for something to move, but nothing happened. He walked a bit more, and a deep growl came from right behind him. Now firmly grabbing his ax, he whirled around but again saw nothing. He began to sweat and his breathing increased.

Christian fumbled around to take his medication, as he wasn't sure whether anxiety was causing his hypersensitivity. He unscrewed the top of one bottle, tilted his head back, and saw a large humanoid shape watching him from atop a house across the street. It was hard to see, and aside from the outline, the figure remained a mystery. But it was there for him. It jumped backward off the roof and out of sight, sending Christian into a frenzy, making him drop his medication all over the sidewalk below.

He ran after it, feeling energized, and scaled a small fence to reach the front of the house. He stopped, ready to attack, and tried to catch his breath. Something sharp scraped against the side of an abandoned house next to him, and he ran into the yard, breaking through the front door. Something ran across the roof as Christian broke through several rotted walls and finally the back door, using brute force. He shot his gaze all around the property, seeing nothing. Sweat dripped down across his face, and he spit it out of his mouth.

"This can't be happening. This isn't real," he said quietly to himself.

A large drop of spit plopped onto his boot. Christian steadied his nerves and looked up. Looming over him was the large shadow, now staring down at him, grunting like a bear. It was massive and could have done anything it wanted to him, but it remained still, as if teasing him.

He pulled out his gun and fired, missing the target as it fled in the blink of an eye. Christian chased it with every last bit of energy he had. After a few minutes, he forgot where he was but kept a close eye on the figure leading him along. It was too fast to be human.

"What is this?" he asked himself in a complete frenzy.

Christian stopped, realizing he was in the graveyard of Alexandra's church, where Caroline was buried. There was a disturbance on the ground ahead of him, and he walked to it cautiously, turning on a flashlight. John Smith's gravestone was broken in half, lying on the ground. On the grass next to it, the words *And that name we fear* were carved into the dirt.

"Oh my God," he muttered to himself, his heart beating painfully in his chest. "He's back."

He then remembered his family and ran home as quickly as he could, bursting into the house and locking all the doors and windows. He checked the areas where he had hidden weapons and yelled for Adam and Rebecca. Rebecca came down in a hurry, very concerned for her husband, and he frantically asked her whether Adam was okay. He continually interrupted her and eventually pushed past, running to Adam's bedroom, kicking the door open.

Adam was asleep and jumped awake, falling off his bed at the commotion.

"What happened? Dad, what is it?"

Christian swallowed hard and questioned everything that just occurred.

"Christian, Jesus Christ. What are you doing?" Rebecca yelled at him, visibly upset.

"I . . . don't . . . know," he said, almost at a total loss for words.

He sat on Adam's bed and apologized for scaring them. He was drenched in sweat and stank of gunpowder.

"What happened? What did you do?" Rebecca asked, fearful of what he'd say.

"Nothing. But something's wrong. Something is very wrong."

"What is it?" she asked.

"Did you check on Alexandra?" he asked Rebecca.

"Yes, we just hung up a few minutes ago. She's fine. What happened?"

"Nothing," he replied, not wanting to worry them yet. "I'm sorry."

"Did you take your medication today?" Adam asked.

Christian didn't answer and went downstairs to be by himself. He didn't remove his armor and just stared out the window, alone. Blackheart was back. This was what he had hoped for all this time, but now he greatly regretted his wish.

16

Final Nightmare

Alexandra fell into a deep sleep that night, unaware of anything that happened to Christian. She had no lingering effects after her problem during the church service, but something felt different now. She entered another dream.

The moonlight brought a muted color to all her possessions in the room. All the windows were open, with the velvety curtains dancing in the wind, inviting in an unexpected visitor.

A man appeared over her, watching with childlike curiosity. He walked to the side of the bed, moving his hand over her foot but not touching it yet. A slight warmth came from his skin. With a soft touch, he walked toward her upper body, letting her legs guide him. Alex was very relaxed and not afraid somehow.

His hand moved gently above her hip and up her arm, paralyzing her. He bent down and sniffed her hair, gently nuzzling her ear. Alexandra tried to wake herself but couldn't. She didn't want to leave the dream.

The man ran his long tongue along her jawline, sending an impulse into Alex she'd never felt before. She rubbed her thighs together, now fully enjoying the sensual experience. She had missed a very important part of early womanhood but understood the sacrifices needed for her career. A mother would have guided her through all these conflicted feelings.

Is this what it's supposed to feel like?

He caressed her neckline with a sharp nail before taking her arm and directing her hand toward him. He had an odd deformation and she realized it was a scar. A large, ugly scar. The scar she gave to Blackheart when she stabbed him in the cemetery.

Alex jumped up from the dream, sexually excited and equally frightened. Her alarm clock was somehow changed to a different station than she set it to and played a very intense song that just added to the uncertainty of what happened.

My lips are full and lovely
You'd do anything to feel them

She pulled her knees to her chest and hugged them, feeling vulnerable. The sensation of the man's scar was still very present on her hands.

Don't just sit in darkness
Let me take the pain away

She began to pray to herself, trying to tune out the song, but it wasn't working.

Mess with me and eat my sanity
Come and taste me please

She finally got the courage to pull the plug out of the wall to silence the radio. She grabbed her house phone and quickly called Rebecca, not sure who else she could talk to about this. She nervously walked downstairs, waiting for Rebecca to pick up, looking around at anything else disturbed in the parsonage. But it all looked normal.

"Hello," Rebecca finally answered.

"Hey, Becca, it's me."

"You don't sound good. Is everything okay?"

"No, it's not."

Suddenly, Christian grabbed the phone and took over the conversation. "Alex, he's back. Listen to me closely . . ."

But Alex dropped the phone as she heard those words and then noticed a disemboweled deer on her doorstep outside. A large vulture was feasting on it. It lifted its ugly head to stare her down before going back to eat. She began trembling and checked that the door was locked. She slid down onto the floor, facing away from the animal, hearing Christian yell for her over the phone. She felt frozen with fear.

"Please, oh God, please, don't let it be true," she said out loud, hoping somehow she was still having a bad dream. But she already knew it was true.

She sat like that for several hours before calling her secretary, Carol, to cancel the church support group for that day.

17

Public Disturbance

Department of Public Works employee Johnny Mays had fifteen years under his belt. He had laughed off the stories everyone told him early on in his career about Mr. Smith, hounds from hell, and everything else. He had risen to the level of parks and grounds supervisor, enjoying a somewhat easy rise to the top. As all the more senior DPW workers saw pay cuts after Blackheart was killed, they started leaving in droves. Out of desperation, the department quickly moved the younger workers to top pay, put them in management positions, and contracted out the rest of the work to various vendors. This was done by Mayor Wiggins to save money, but DPW superintendent Dan Mathews disagreed with him wholeheartedly on the matter. Because of their close friendship, it never became a debate but was just accepted.

Earlier in the day, Mays was told to go investigate several complaints of a foul odor on Chrysanthemum Drive. After his hour-long coffee break to start the morning, he took his shiny new town vehicle to the location and saw the contractors already on-site. They were almost always late, so he was shocked to see them on time.

He parked the truck and noticed none of the men were working but rather just staring up at the trees. He cautiously walked over to the group and asked what the issue was. One man pointed up, and Johnny looked up to see countless animals slaughtered and hung all over the trees. The smell was horrid, so he quickly covered his face with his sleeve. The droplets of remaining blood struck the ground like drizzling raindrops.

"What the hell happened here?" he asked, but no one responded.

Johnny looked further up on the dirt road and saw a pile of dead animals blocking the way to Blackheart's house. The heap was no less than ten feet tall and wide. There were mainly larger animals, like bear, coyotes, and a few bucks, but it was hard to see everything in the pile.

Everyone went around and up to the top of the hill toward the collapsed mansion. The wreckage was moved around, revealing a cement underground cellar with handfuls of large trees knocked over all around the property.

"Just like it used to be," the one worker said to himself.

Johnny realized that the stories might have been true. There was a monster loose in the town. He quickly called the superintendent to report his findings, who then alerted Mayor Wiggins. They deliberated whether to address the situation at tonight's town council meeting, but the mayor chose not to, as it would affect the town's anniversary celebration.

18

Ignored Warning

That night, the monthly town council meeting commenced. Attending were four council members—all Meadowsville lifelong residents—Mayor Chazz Wiggins, Police Chief Flynn, Fire Chief Hatfield, and DPW Superintendent Dan Mathews. Unlike previous incarnations, these meetings were now civil and more informational. Mayor Wiggins was a first-term mayor and truly cared for the town. He was a big part of the progressive changes made to Meadowsville in the last few years. Knowing the in-depth history of the town, he used the motto *Come Chat with Chazz* to entice people to take him up on his open-door policy and completely distance himself from past administrations.

Because the mayor adequately managed the new department heads, there were very few complaints coming across his desk, which was exactly how he liked to see things operate. There were some residents who didn't like how he pushed out the prior supervisors in each department, but he had made it his utmost priority and accomplished it in a short period of time after being elected. He, like everyone else, was very excited about the town's 125th anniversary celebration the following day.

Low-level chatter filled the room before the mayor stood at the decades-old podium. "Good evening, everyone. How are you all tonight?"

There was no response.

"Come on, folks, give me something here."

Most of the people smiled and giggled.

"Tomorrow night is going to be something special. This town celebrates its one hundred and twenty-fifth anniversary. It's had a rich history. Some good and some bad. But, beyond it all, we're all here together. Without spoiling any surprises, I want to thank our planning board, Jordan, Juliet, and Jenny."

The three stood up and everyone applauded them.

"And to my good friend Dan Mathews and all his men at public works. They continue to keep this town spotless and have been a huge help getting the event set up for tomorrow. Let's give them all a hand."

Mayor Wiggins clapped along with the crowd again, all genuinely happy to be there that evening. He started to speak again when the large wooden entryway doors swung open. In walked an unkempt-looking Christian in full armor.

The crowd grew silent, unsure of his intentions. The rumors about him being a crazed alcoholic were well-known.

Christian slowly looked around, fury in his eyes. He walked to the secondary podium, facing the mayor to address the administration. Rebecca and Adam crept in behind him and sat in the back row of the chambers, highly embarrassed.

"Christian Reed, everyone. Meadowsville's living legend," the mayor said, clapping nervously with almost no one else joining him.

"Mayor Wiggins, I don't mean to interrupt this meeting, but I have something important to tell everyone. He's back."

"Who?"

"Blackheart," Christian said.

Everyone looked at each other, assuming he was intoxicated.

"Go home, you drunk," someone yelled from the crowd.

Christian ignored it, staying focused on Wiggins.

"Now, now. There's no need for that," the mayor said, trying to keep control of everyone. "Christian, it's been a long time since all that happened. And we are all very proud of what you did for this town. You saved it from the brink of destruction and killed that man. 'Things have changed' . . . those were your words."

"He wasn't a man, and it's all starting to happen again."

"Okay, you killed him. And you graciously patrol the town every night to make sure things stay safe. He can't come back."

"But he is."

"Mr. Smith is dead. You killed him with your own hands."

"Blackheart."

"Excuse me?"

"His name is Blackheart," Christian responded, hearing a few audience members laugh.

"Okay then. Blackheart. There have been no signs of foul play. No murders or missing persons. Nothing out of the norm," the mayor said, knowing it was a lie, and he felt sick saying it.

"You're wrong."

"Okay, so how does a dead man come back? And why after all this time?"

"I don't know. All I know is he's here and we have to act before it's too late."

"What do you recommend?"

"I need the entire police force and—"

Police Chief Flynn cut in. "We don't take orders from a citizen. Especially not one whose mental health is highly questionable. My men allow you to wander around each and every night because we're still hanging onto the one thing you did fifteen years ago. That is the extent I am willing to stretch my department."

Mayor Wiggins put up his hands and tried to steer the meeting back onto a less argumentative track.

"Okay. Christian, I will have the police continue their due diligence and patrol Chrysanthemum Drive more often. If you see anything out of the ordinary, please call them and let them know."

"Have it your way. You've been warned," Christian said sternly before leaving.

Rebecca and Adam quickly followed after him, fighting the urge to cover their faces.

19

Anniversary Celebration

The town celebration went on as scheduled the following day. Almost every resident was in attendance. They all enjoyed each other's company as the Dead Heads played loudly. The smell of cheeseburgers, funnel cakes, and cotton candy permeated the nighttime air. The spirited screams of children riding on the Ferris wheel and carousel were loud and clear, and even the teenagers were enjoying the shooting games and bumper cars. It was a sweet sight from a community that spent so much time fractured.

Alexandra walked around, faking interest and pretending to be having fun, but she hadn't been out of the house in days. Since the issue at her front door, and after she and Christian confirmed with one another that Blackheart had returned, she didn't know what else to do. She got inundated with support group members asking her when their next meeting would be, and she did her best to get away to a new topic. She struggled with being unable to meet their needs due to her own personal circumstances.

Christian and his family caught up with her. Rebecca hugged her hard and asked how she was. Christian was cleaned up but still in armor and looking around frantically. He hadn't slept in days. Adam asked to go see some of his friends, and Christian and Rebecca let him go. He needed to be away from his parents after everything that was going on recently.

Mayor Wiggins joined the band on stage and pretended to play with them. They slapped hands and stepped to the side. "Thank you all for being here tonight," he yelled.

A loud *Meadowsville* chant began, and the mayor encouraged it.

"Yes! That's right. This town is a great place to be. Now I wanted to take a few minutes to go over this town's history. One hundred and twenty-five years ago, several families founded this town. The Smiths, Martins, Fitzpatricks, and Bensons, who still have lineage here today. I know, we're all familiar with the name *Smith*. But he was a founding member of this town. He and the others named this vast area Meadowsville to reflect its size, openness, and beauty. This would eventually lead to each street being named symbolically by the following generations. Friendship, success, and positivity are just some of those meanings, which is what this place is all about. Each street and each set of citizens are unique and special.

"Over time, this rural area became appealing to other families, who began to migrate here. In the following decades, we welcomed medical centers, small businesses, restaurants, bowling alleys, schools, and everything a person could want or need in one place. All from our diverse citizens and their efforts. And we all thank everyone for making this place what is."

The crowd screamed in support, and the mayor continued. Christian sensed something in the air, something indescribable but alarming. He began to walk around, gently bumping into everyone by accident, trying to locate whatever it was.

"And this town reached an economic success like never before under the guidance of former Mayor Wilkins. Then the reign of John Smith took us over, leading us into a very corrupt and dark time. With Christian Reed's help, we overcame that period, and we thank him for his service."

Everyone began cheering and looked for Christian, who had left the crowd. Then a *John Smith* chant started, almost like a loyal cult. Christian and Alex felt the energy, and both independently realized Blackheart had returned because the town brought him back. The energy and recognition of his presence gave him power. His manipulation of Alexandra resurrected him with her Easter prayer, giving him access through her dreams. That was the last bit of power Blackheart needed. And he was here with them right now.

They all began speaking Smith's poem like a prayer as Christian ran back in, pleading for everyone to stop.

And that name we fear is Mr. Smith!
And that name we fear is Mr. Smith!
And that name we fear is Mr. Smith!
And that name we fear is . . .

Before the crowd finished the chant, all the lights went off and the crowd was left in darkness, silencing them. A moment later, the fireworks began, illuminating the stage. A body hung from the awning—former Mayor Wilkins, dead and bloodied. Mayor Wiggins quickly hopped off the stage.

A large banner reading *Blackheart* written in Mayor Wilkins's blood hung over the stage below a large group of vultures who calmly surveyed the crowd. And the man, the legend, this town's Blackheart stood tall on the stage. Showing more signs of being an evolved entity, his appearance had been altered, but he was still recognizable. He looked slightly aged, now wearing a dark red suit, holding a silver walking stick with a wooden serpent wrapped around it. He laid his leatherbound glove comfortably on it, as if waiting for someone to dance with at a ball.

Blackheart began to speak loudly enough for everyone to hear him, not needing a microphone to carry his powerful voice. "And the name that you should all fear . . . is Blackheart," he growled out, sending the petrified crowd into frenzied hysterics.

The fireworks continued to go off, beginning to shoot in all directions, hitting people and lighting the stage on fire. The vultures descended and started pecking at random crowd members, causing everyone to scramble. Mayor Wilkins's body fell into Blackheart's arms. He looked at it briefly before flinging it at Mayor Wiggins, knocking him down.

Alexandra screamed for Rebecca, who was swept away in the crowd, and then Blackheart suddenly appeared within feet of Alexandra, watching her intently and serenading her with distressing song lyrics.

Do you mind if I hurt you
Beg for mercy, it won't help

Now she couldn't see him, but she heard him.

I've waited for someone like you
Kept on believing . . .

She saw him again in the crowd—he was the only one not running.

I wish I had some other choice
But I now have to kill you

She lost him again but then felt him breathe on her from behind.

Look what you've done
I'm here for you. Just for you.

She turned to see him face-to-face and felt every ounce of herself in jeopardy.

Christian managed to reach them and tackled Blackheart. They rolled into an open patch of grass, seeing only each other as the fireworks continue to explode overhead. Christian held Blackheart by the neck and punched him relentlessly, fracturing parts of his skull with each strike. Blood poured out, covering Christian, who embraced it. He yelled like a wild hunter and continued destroying his enemy, taking out all his frustrations on Blackheart, who lay there, smiling at him and not resisting or fighting back, as if entertained by the onslaught. They held eye contact throughout.

Christian went for his ax but couldn't reach it. Blackheart didn't react much at all but then turned to stare at Alex, longing for her help as Christian did his best to hurt the beast.

She felt his request, like an injured animal. No words were needed. She once again felt him inside her. She couldn't stop looking back at him and began to feel remorseful. He wasn't fighting back. He was an evil creature, but violence wasn't the answer. It didn't work fifteen years ago and wouldn't work this time. He was back because he needed to be. The town wanted him here. And if she were stronger, she could have kept him away from her. She possibly could have prevented his return.

Christian fumbled at his equipment, as he couldn't stop himself from bloodying the monster. He called for Alex to give him his ax, but she was frozen in thought.

Blackheart looked at her and mouthed the words *Help me.*

Just like in her dream, she saw his now green eyes and remembered David's face when he'd first come into her life. Bloodied, in pain, and needing help.

She recalled her father telling her once, "You have to learn to see the good in everyone. As hard as it may be. Even the most sinful and wicked ones. They need the most love and compassion."

She kicked the ax away and tried to pull Christian off, yelling at him to stop. Christian shoved her down and grabbed his pistol, aiming it at Blackheart's face. Alexandra quickly got to her feet and pushed his arm up, causing the bullet to disappear into the night sky. Christian yanked his arm away from her and stood over her like an angry parent. Blackheart lay there like a dead body before getting to his feet and leaping away into the darkness. Christian tried to chase, but Alex restrained him again.

"Goddammit! Let me go. What the fuck are you doing?" he yelled, trying to get away from her.

"Christian, stop it. Let him be!"

Christian tried to see his prey, now long gone.

He finally freed himself from Alex's grasp. "You just killed this town, you fucking idiot. Did you forget who that is? Where's your fuckin' head at!"

"Don't you dare speak to me like that," she fought back.

Rebecca finally found Adam, hugging him and thanking God he wasn't harmed. Adam was angry she didn't find him faster, but he was relieved she was there now. He was even more irate that his father left them both in harm's way again.

They saw the dispute between Alex and Christian and rushed over to them.

"This won't solve anything," Alexandra tried to reason.

"I could've killed him. I can't believe you. You're so fuckin' stupid!"

Alex started crying, filled with confusion and anger, and ran off. Rebecca arrived, heard her husband's harsh words, and slapped Christian in the face, reprimanding him for speaking to Alex like that. He raised a hand to hit back but stopped himself. He took his ax and threw it a good distance, screaming in frustration. He walked away from his family, retrieving his cherished weapon and taking it with him. Both Rebecca and Adam were shocked at his behavior and devastated he had left them.

20

Teachable Moment

Fifteen years before, Alexandra and Father Richard had gone home to their parsonage after David arrived at their church for the first time.

"Dad, why would you take him in? Did you see the blood all over him? We don't know where he's been or what he's done," Alex said, scolding her father.

Father Richard just looked at her, keeping his composure.

"He might hurt us. Is any of this getting through?"

"Alexandra," her father began. "You will learn, as you go off to your schooling, that empathy is probably the most important thing a good leader needs to possess."

She calmed herself a bit and began to listen more closely.

"David found us. He has no one else. No home. No way to survive. He's afraid and confused. He's at his lowest point. Do you think we should send him off to certain death?"

She shook her head reluctantly.

"It is our job to be there for those who need us. We don't decide who God brings to us. We just have to trust we're meeting each individual at a crucial point in their lives, and we can aide them in keeping their faith and living in His name. We learn from them as much as they learn from us."

She sat deep in thought, questioning his poor judgment about David.

"You have to learn to see the good in everyone. As hard as it may be. Even the most sinful and wicked ones. They need the most love and compassion."

Alexandra would later question how much of this advice from her father was meant for Blackheart.

21

Gentle Reminder

Christian stormed away from the fairgrounds after the chaos at the town's anniversary celebration. He was very angry at his wife and Alexandra. He patrolled around town in a fury, pushing over trash cans and yelling. He became a one-man wrecking crew, taking out his frustrations on anything he could get his hands on. The town was quiet, and everyone was now home with doors and windows locked, fearful of Blackheart's return. Christian felt in control again. This was how things should be. This was what he had wanted all this time. The anger made him feel alive.

There was no sign of Blackheart anywhere. Christian went home to collect more weapons and continue hunting. He was so irate that his vision was blurred. He had skipped his medication for several days, so he was fighting past the withdrawal effects and increased anxiety symptoms.

As he got closer to his house, he heard loud music playing. As he was in sight of his home, he saw the front door wide open with the music coming from inside. He pulled up his ax, peering in all the base-level windows, looking for anything inside.

I know you're there
You're hiding from me

He slowly looked in the front door.

I hear you getting closer
I know what you want

He stealthily entered the house, going through the downstairs, keeping his back to the walls, sweat pouring off his forehead. Nothing seemed out of sorts.

This is open season
And I won't let you get far

Still finding nothing, he ascended the stairway leading to the bedrooms. The music got louder with each step he took.

You have to put the blame elsewhere
Blame your confusion on another

He looked into Caroline's room, left the way she kept it. Someone had laid out complete outfits for both Rebecca and

Adam across the floor, perfectly aligned to be worn. Blackheart had not only invaded his home but was telling Christian he could give Rebecca and Adam the same fate as Caroline.

Can you feel your hope dwindle
You won't win this time

The radio played next to the outfits and Christian stomped it, stopping the music. He was satisfied with the feeling of bloodlust. His mission was clear. He rationalized all his past actions. He was never crazy. He was the only one who knew this would happen. And he was the only one ready for it. The threat from Blackheart now sent him over the edge.

22

Brutal Honesty

Days later, Alex finished up her long-overdue support group, and the entire session was about the fear everyone felt over Blackheart coming back. She tried to preach God's love and the power of prayer, but neither the attendees nor even she was convinced of the sentiments.

All the members left at noon, and she was alone at the altar. She looked up at the familiar face of Jesus Christ in the stained-glass window, praying for help. The doors opened and she didn't need to look back, because she already felt Blackheart's presence. She turned to face him.

He slowly walked toward her, unscathed, as if Christian had never touched him. They stared at one another, unsure what would happen. She wished she could call for help, but no one was anywhere near the church.

"It must be hard," Blackheart calmly said to her, casually leaning back on the front pew, extending his cane in front of him. The silver glistened and the eyes of the wooden snake looked up at Jesus. "To take on all these people's problems as your own."

"No one else can . . ." she muttered.

He looks at her hands, not seeing a wedding ring or sign of a significant other. He could feel her desperation and loneliness. He smelled it like a hungry dog would a piece of meat.

"And to do it by yourself. Takes a strong person. A truly special individual."

Alex stayed quiet, trying to remember her father's words, but she struggled spiritually with doing so.

"You're more special than you know, Alexandra," he said. He was the only person aside from her father who called her by her full name. "I doubt anyone tells you that. All you hear is sorrow and sadness and distress." He paused briefly. "If only someone else knew just how special you were. To appreciate you as much as you deserve. To commend you for just being you."

Her eyes became glossy and a tear fell down her cheek. As much as she tried to deny it, he was right, and she knew it.

"I always had to depend on loneliness. It's safe. It never leaves you. It always understands you. Do you know that feeling?" Blackheart said.

She stayed quiet and recalled David saying something very similar. She again noticed Blackheart's now greenish eyes. It made her very nostalgic for David.

"No one could handle being with me. The lifestyle is too different. They just never quite got it."

Alex thought of all her attempts at dating and each person losing interest and not even trying to understand her life choices.

"You hurt so many people. It's different," she countered.

"You're right. I've made my mistakes. A lot of them. All I can do now is repent and try to do better. If only someone could help me do that. To bring me closer to God," he said, inadvertently hinting at his intentions.

"You killed David and the others . . ."

"David . . . was someone I really cared for. I watched over him for ten long years before I had to save him from himself. I did what I thought was best. Did you know he was going to take his own life? That's an unforgiveable sin, isn't it? I just couldn't let him. I wouldn't have been able to live with myself."

Alex teared up more, wishing more than ever that David was back. This conversation with Blackheart was the most meaningful one she's had with anyone in a long time. He seemed to really understand her.

"I really did want to save him, and I ended up hurting him. Just like everyone else. Things went too far, and I wasn't able to stop it. And now I have to live this long, tragic life with all those evil deeds on my mind. And on top of those terrible things that were done to me by John Smith. Those kinds of scars never heal."

Alex swallowed hard, fighting her anxiety.

"I was so young. And the three core things all children believe in were stripped from me. Parent's love, faith in God, and trust. Gone. And the trauma overwhelmed me for a long time. Then I spent so much time living for other people and putting them before myself. This town and everyone in it. They needed me. And I adhered to what they needed me to be. But all that time, I ignored my own problems. All because I wasn't ready to face my own personal demons. And that was a mistake too. But this town can do that to you. They'll take everything out of you and still want more. They don't care about you. They only care about what you can do for them."

Alexandra bit her upper lip hard to stop herself from fully sobbing at the trueness of his words.

"But through everything, I've had the last fifteen years to reflect on my misdeeds and ask for forgiveness."

"This is so confusing. Why did you come back? How?"

"I'm back because you all need me to be here. Meadowsville needed me to restore balance here again. I want to finally help them all, and you, in the process. Together we can make a difference. Together we can evolve."

Alexandra turned her head, refusing the notion of his attempt to be genuine.

"I understand your reluctance. You're very smart, and the last thing I want to do is force you into anything you're not ready for. All I ask is that you give me, a lost soul, a chance."

Alex softened at his self-degradation, wiped her eyes, and nodded quietly. Somehow Blackheart was able to accurately and deeply extend compassion to her in a way she hadn't felt since David—he had also come to her in a very similar situation, and it turned out to be one of the most meaningful events of her young life. As outlandish and bewildering as it sounded, maybe this was the opportunity she had been waiting for. Blackheart might have been the one who could finally help her. And she could help him find a new path too. All this time, God might have been preparing her this unorthodox situation. Maybe David wasn't the endpoint but rather something to prepare her.

Blackheart smiled at her with perfect, sharpened teeth and began to leave. He noticed a radio in the back of the church and snapped his fingers, putting on one of Alex's favorite female-lead songs.

I will die if you want me to
I will cry if you need me to
I would be hurt for you
I would kill for you
You're just like me
I can wash away your pain . . .

Alexandra smiled as he left the building, at his care, understanding, and willingness to change. She was also very proud of how strong she was during this tense time, all without anyone else's help. Even a small confidence-boosting experience like this meant a lot to her. She began to digest the concept that she was stronger and more capable than she knew. And much to her dismay, she had Blackheart to thank for it.

23

Family Conflict

The next day, Christian pulled up to the front doors at Meadowsville High School. He was exhausted and distressed. He hadn't spoken to Rebecca or Alexandra in days or slept at all. He had kept watch over the house to ensure his family's safety but hadn't stayed there. He hoped to at least explain himself to Adam and start repairing their relationship. Rebecca was a more sensitive matter and would require the proper timing and approach.

He looked inside the school and saw paintings of Blackheart hung around the lockers. He got out of the car and walked in aggressively, pushing past several people. All the students stared as he started pulling down the images piece by piece and yelling at the kids leaving the school.

"Is this funny? You guy think this is a joke? Your lives are at risk and you treat this like a game," he yelled, kicking at the crumbled-up art on the floor.

Adam walked down the hall, embarrassed once again at seeing his father confront his peers and make a scene. This was it. He couldn't stand it any longer.

"What the hell are you doing?" he yelled at Christian, causing him to stop and everyone around to gawk.

Christian pulled down one more piece, unable to control his anger.

"Dad, stop it! You're obsessed," Adam barked out, finally getting his father's full attention.

Christian stood over him.

"You want truth? You wanna hear someone finally wake you up? You should've been home all those years ago. You should've been there to protect us, but you weren't. You were doing this same kind of bullshit. And Caroline is dead because of it."

Christian teared up and softened at the truthful words.

"And you left us in that crowd the other night. It's always about what you need. It's never about us. We're an afterthought to you, you selfish son of a bitch. Mom is afraid to say all this, but I'm not."

Christian shed a tear as Adam put him in his place.

"You're a shitty father, a laughingstock to this town, and an even worse vigilante. News flash—you never did kill that fucking thing. So the last fifteen years . . . all the accolades and all that crap . . . all a lie. You're a fucking joke, and you make

Mom and me so embarrassed. We hate you for it!" Adam clapped sarcastically in Christian's face, pushing past his father and knocking him over, leaving the school with several of his friends.

One of the teachers asked Christian to leave immediately, and he did, feeling heartbroken. He felt quarantined like an animal, and while he wanted to be upset at his son's blistering barrage, he focused his attention on Blackheart again.

After speaking with Adam about the incident, Rebecca left Christian a voicemail telling him not to come home until he was ready to apologize to both of them and get his act together.

Defeating that monster once and for all was the only way Christian assumed he could win back the town's admiration and his family's respect too.

24

Attempt Thwarted

Feeling lost and worried that he had no one left to support his cause, Christian went to see Alex, the only other person who could understand his position. Even after she stopped him from killing the creature the other night, she'd battled Blackheart alongside him and knew the true nature of the beast and the imminent danger of him being back in Meadowsville. He walked into Meadowsville Community Church and tried to give Alex a hug, but she blocked him from doing so.

"Alex, I'm sorry. I shouldn't have said those awful things. I just don't want you or anyone else to get hurt. Blackheart is no good, and he's just going to go back to his old ways."

"I don't think so," she said.

"What?"

"I think he's changed."

Christian lost his patience very quickly and began yelling at her again. "He came to you. I knew I smelled him in here," Christian surmised. "What did he say to you?"

Alexandra didn't respond.

"No, no, no . . . this is what he does. He's a—a proficient manipulator. He's done it so many times to so many people. It's like second nature to him now. He got into your head. And you let him."

"How can you be so sure?"

"Look at his track record. What are you thinking? You saw what he did to us. To David. To this town. And you're enabling it," Christian said, losing patience with her. "You're risking your life like your brain took a vacation. And for what? So you can have a friend?"

Anger bubbled in Alexandra and she stood up to him, no longer fearing him. She rejected his abuse and, for the first time, she was ready to fight.

"I will not be spoken to like that," she yelled, silencing Christian, who was surprised at the outburst.

"Alex, I just don't get what you're doing."

"I'm doing the right thing, Christian. And I'm no longer concerned whether you approve or not." She fought back tears and shortness of breath from the raw emotion.

They looked at each other. They had been so close for so long and now were at odds.

"Have it your way then," he responded, ending the heated discussion and gathering himself to leave.

"Christian, go home and take care of your family. They need you more than this town does," she called out to him.

He stopped, taking great offense to being told what to do. "I appreciate the advice from someone who can't even get a second date. Good luck with your new friend, Alexandra. You call me when he's got your fuckin' neck in his mouth."

She came down off the altar and confronted him again. "Don't you dare disrespect me or this church like that. Now get out and don't come back!" she exclaimed, unable to hold back her tears.

Christian, having lost his connection with everyone he held dear, reverted to his anger again. He walked toward the front doors. "You just remember that when I find him—and I will—I will end it once and for all," he called out, kicking the doors open.

Several hours passed and Alex sat in a pew, completely distraught and feeling abandoned.

At noon, once again, Blackheart entered. He approached her and hugged her. No words were needed. She didn't even try to resist the kind gesture—she embraced it. She had no fight left in her. And he could sense that.

"It's okay. We don't have to talk now," he said, almost cradling her.

They sat like this for several minutes, and Alexandra was able to regain her composure. She looked at Blackheart, who took one of his nails and collected the final tear coming out of her left eye. He examined it with her before gently letting it drip from the jagged edge of his nail. His intense eyes met hers, and Alexandra felt an even stronger nonverbal communication with him. She hugged him back and enjoyed the comfort of being with someone who was concerned for her. She thought again of David and recalled when he had kissed her before departing. His lips were so soft and inviting. The thought of it made her heart quiver.

Blackheart and Alexandra held each other in the quiet church. Fifteen years of loneliness almost completely gone in one instance. Alex looked at him again. He was watching the stained-glass window of Jesus with fear in his eyes. He had changed. He was ready to be better.

His mighty hands caressed her body, just like in her last dream. She fell into a trance, unable to resist his strong embrace. With no pain, one of his nails gently lacerated her forearm. He licked the blood off without her noticing, as her eyes had fallen shut in the overwhelming comfort she experienced. He began speaking lyrics into her ear, another one of Alex's favorite songs.

We can be like the seasons
Changing for the greater good.

Alexandra quietly sang back, following his lead.

Take me by the hand,
We can fly together,

He joined back in, almost stifling her attempt.

And become one.

She tried to join back in, but again he sang over her.

Don't fear me
Never, ever fear me
Say goodbye to sadness

Alex finally came to her right mind and realized the position she was in. A small trail of blood dripped off her forearm onto the red rug of the church. She looked back up at Blackheart, who again stared at the stained-glass window with a very mild smile, her blood outlining his exaggerated mouth. His eyes had reverted back to blue.

This was *not* David. This was nothing like David. Blackheart was no longer serenading and now seemed intent on mocking the depiction on Jesus Christ, as if he had tricked the system and planned to use Alex to see his master plan through.

Christian was right. Blackheart had been manipulating her this entire time, taking advantage of her loneliness, grief over David, and everything else. He was no different than before. He was using her as a pawn in some unholy war against God.

"You're as close to God as I can get."

She remembered the words from fifteen years ago.

The two sat quietly for another moment. She was completely uncomfortable now and tried to get back to her feet.

"I can't do this. I won't do this," she said to him, finally moving away and retreating to the altar, which represented a safe haven of sorts, directly under Jesus Christ.

Blackheart began to morph into a ghastly new appearance. His eyes sank in and turned pitch-black, and his mouth expanded so much the skin around it split and peeled back, protruding a bit. His perfect teeth were now jagged and sloppily sticking out. His suit was left in shreds and his cane was snapped in half like a toothpick.

He took on a new appearance, more feral. He was as terrifying as she remembered. The pews around him were pushed back, making room for his now hulking size. The scar on his shoulder opened up a bit as his physical size increased. The hundreds of other scars, encompassing his gnarled body, stretched and had random patches of hair growing out of them. Some had begun to split open, leaving subtle blood trails down his body. He grew to almost double his original size, and Alex stood there wondering how much worse he could appear.

The monster roared so loudly that all the windows shattered all except the largest one with Jesus on it. A flock of vultures suddenly flew around the building, squawking loudly. Blackheart sneered at her but seemed to hold himself back from attacking.

"I can't believe how close you got. This is what you do. Christian was right. You get into people's heads and make them think they need you, that they can't live without you. That's how you got those women to listen to you. That's how you got David and everyone else. And you're using me to get to God."

He stood smirking at her as foamy saliva dripped from his mouth like a rabid animal.

"But you're still afraid of Him. That's your weakness. That'll always be your weakness." She finally understood why her father would not stand down to the monster—because he knew the same truth.

In a very deep, raspy voice, Blackheart responded, "The blood of this town is on your hands. I'll save you for last. You're too important to me to waste."

Blackheart roared again and leapt out the remaining window. Shards of Jesus crashed down, cutting him, but it went unnoticed by the creature.

Alex stood tall, no longer crying but furious and determined to end the terror. She was the only one who could do it. Her path had never been in the hands of Blackheart. He was simply a stepping-stone for her to realize her full potential. And now she was ready for it. God was working through Blackheart, and He didn't even realize it. It all started to make sense now.

25

Complete Destruction

Blackheart arrived in town, no longer weakened by the sunlight. He was a new type of monster now. An advanced evil. The rules and limitations of his former life no longer affected him.

The vultures followed him, circling overhead as he killed random citizens he came across. He didn't try to drink their blood or taste their flesh. He just laid waste to them like garbage and continued on.

He passed a cell phone tower and grabbed the base with his huge hands, knocking it over with a tremendous feat of strength. Electric arcs and sparks provided as good of a light show as the town's fireworks the night he had returned. He roared into the afternoon sky, sending all residents within miles clamoring to find safety as a huge fire started from the damaged tower.

First responders showed up at once due to the lack of other calls, as Blackheart intended. Using one of his oldest, most revered strategies, Blackheart began slaughtering them one by one, waiting for more police, fire, and EMS workers to come by and meet the same fate. The vultures continued to watch from above as the sun beat down on the corpses laid across the ground. He then pulled off the tires of the fire truck and tossed them like toys into nearby buildings, turning the immediate area into a warzone.

The town remained panicked, and dozens of parents scrambled to pick up their children at the town's elementary schools, only to find the teachers overwhelmed or torn to pieces and their kids missing.

Blackheart moved toward the police headquarters. Officers confronted him, and he killed them one by one with ease, absorbing their bullets like gusts of wind. As a group of five officers surrounded him, he leaped into the air and put his hands and feet through the chests of four of them, landing on the fifth and effortlessly biting a gaping hole in his neck. The officer squirmed on the ground for a few seconds as his blood oozed out. Blackheart watched him die but took no pleasure in it as he once had. He spit out the skin as the vultures squawked loudly, almost laughing at the butchery.

Blackheart began smashing the police cars in front of all the entrances and exits, blocking in the staff members and igniting small fires around the building. He took off, leaping across town and destroying the police substations, the fire stations, and every other means of help for the citizens, one by one. Meadowsville's first responders were now unable to help as this evil went about completing his master plan.

26

Validation

Christian had not gone home but continued to patrol the streets. Unaware of the full attack on the town, he came upon a one police substation and saw several officers trapped inside. He tried to get to them but was unable to move the wreckage.

His adrenaline rose because Blackheart was behind it. It was time to show everyone why Christian wasn't a useless town drunk. With almost superhuman strength, he used his ax to chop through the side entrance, enabling the officers to crawl out. Luckily, they were okay. Their radios went off and told them to report to town hall immediately. The police thanked Christian and got into one of the only surviving patrol cars.

A dark limo pulled up behind Christian, and one of the town council members asked him to get in. He entered without hesitation, and they began to maneuver through the chaotic streets. The various fires all over town had darkened the sky. They passed destroyed property and other areas about to succumb to the carnage of Blackheart. The town looked just like it did fifteen years ago, and Christian felt a new instability that combined all his feelings into one scary and dangerous mindset. The town needed him to save it.

They arrived at their destination, and both the councilman and Christian ran into the town hall and then the mayor's office. The hallways were lined with police officers and firefighters who appeared burned, dirtied, injured, and exhausted. They all waited for orders.

Christian rushed into a closed-door meeting with the mayor.

"Christian, I'm glad you're here. I first off want to apologize for not believing you. On behalf of everyone who doubted you, we're sorry."

Christian spit on the ground, not accepting the apology.

"Okay, well, your creature is destroying the town. You now have all the resources we can give you to do whatever's necessary. Do what needs to be done to protect the town," Mayor Wiggins said, looking very fearful.

"Why should I help you now?" Christian asked. "You thought I was just an annoying public nuisance. Some stupid drunk asshole you guys laughed at in these kinds of closed-door meetings."

"Christian, I never thought of you that way. Honestly. And I never agreed with those who criticized you. This isn't the time to pad your ego though. Please help us. We need you."

"I heard about the scene on Chrysanthemum Drive. Why didn't you tell anyone?"

"I don't know. I was afraid of what it would do. To the people, the celebration, all of it. It was a bad move."

"You're telling me. I could've neutralized this thing before it showed you the same respect it showed Wilkins. You wanna hang from the next stage?"

Wiggins pursed his lips, angry about the sarcastic jabs. He knew the longer they both sat there, the more people were getting hurt.

Christian stood, unsure whether to lead his own war against Blackheart or accept the offer.

Mayor Wiggins got antsy. "You ever know the real story behind Mayor Wilkins? She was arrested and blamed for everything that happened. Chief Jones got her locked up for the rest of her life. Well, until your monster got ahold of her. But Jones only did that because he knew she wouldn't be reelected, and he would be out of a job and most likely charged for being a part of what went on. So he got her indicted, absolved himself completely, and kept himself as department head for several more years before he died."

"Why are you telling me this? They were all careless pricks. And from the sound of it, you're following in the same footsteps."

"I'm sorry, Christian. Goddammit, put your ego aside for a minute. You spent the last fifteen years wishing for this, and now it's here. You have everything you wanted or could need to wage this war. Your war. And those people in the old administration were animals. No better than your Blackheart. That's how they all existed alongside each other so perfectly. They enabled each other. And the past few administrations before me were glorified footnotes who tried to follow suit but failed to go in either direction. That's been the pattern for a long time. I'm nothing like that. I made a bad call, and I own it. I care for this place as much as you do. And I can't do much to save it right now. I need you. We need you. And either you're going to help or you're not. Answer now."

Christian smirked, accepting the plea, and slapped the mayor's desk with his dirty hands, denting the soft wood of its construction. He left the office, ordering a large group of officers to go protect his family and the others to meet him at Chrysanthemum Drive.

Mayor Wiggins got up and punched the wall, mad at himself for not doing anything with the disturbance on Chrysanthemum Drive days before the town's anniversary party and genuinely sorry for his poor judgment. He now saw how easy it was to let things like this get out of control.

27

Clarity

Alexandra, feeling fully empowered for the first time in her life, stood before her congregation later that night. She held service as a way to make up for canceling so many support groups recently. Her people needed her, and she could now be there for them. Her church became a protected sanctuary for them. The countless frightened faces energized her. She was ready to give her first full sermon, no longer accepting interruptions for any reason. She now understood Blackheart in a way no one else did—as a God-fearing creature. And she could use that to defeat him.

"In Genesis 1:1, God made the heavens and the earth. Adam was made on day six, and he was given total ownership over Eden, except for one tree. He became lonely and was given Eve, made with one of his ribs. They live in pure bliss and total ignorance. A serpent came along and manipulated Eve. It promised Eve she'd be God-like if she tasted the forbidden fruit. If she went against her intuition and just listened to him, she would be better off. So she made the mistake of doing his bidding and ate the forbidden fruit from that tree. This was man's original sin.

"But that wasn't because of the devil, who disguised himself as a slithering snake. You see, he was, in actuality, a servant of God. He was put before Eve to test her faith. To act on God's behalf as His prosecutor. Satan actually translates to *accuser*, as seen in the book of Job. So he is not inherently evil but rather God's messenger. He puts special people through difficult events to see whether they keep their faith. Because faith is not meant to be created from these types of circumstances but rather reinforced and strengthened to support someone through it and beyond. The devil is what each person needs him to be. A shape-shifting, constantly evolving entity. The closest experience we will have to hell on this earth. But he, like all things in creation, is still under the watchful eye of God.

"So Adam and Eve were cast out after the fruit was eaten. They now felt pain and tragedy and were seemingly lost, no longer allowed to walk with God. But was mankind doomed forever? Were they too far gone to be saved?"

The crowd watched her, eagerly waiting her conclusion to guide them through this horrific night in Meadowsville.

"No. Of course not. God put His only son here to be with us. To perish for us. Jesus was crucified and died to save us from our transgressions. He restored our ability to find salvation to walk with Him again. Even if we falter, God will always be there to love us unconditionally. Now and forever. The holy spirit lives within each and every one of us, and we need it to prevail against all odds.

"This night, our town is under attack once again. And we need one another, and our beliefs, to get through. Meadowsville, stay strong and stay faithful on this night. And when we reach the end, we will finally be on a righteous path. Amen."

She received a staggering, sincere applause from a now invigorated crowd. Everyone hugged each other, some cried, but all remained together and resilient against the monster they had brought back.

Some left and others remained in-house as Alexandra kept the doors open for all to come in. She had no more fear. She wanted Blackheart to come back to her, as he promised earlier. As she left the podium and hugged her congregation, Christian was there and gave her the biggest hug she'd ever had, apologizing repeatedly for what he had done and said to her. She responded in kind, and both reestablished their caring relationship once again.

"We brought him back. We all did. We wished for this," she told him.

"I know. But it's not too late. I have a plan. Let him come to me," he told her.

"What plan?"

"Trust me."

"Christian, please listen to me. You won't win. It's not like before. Things are different now. You won't be able to kill him with weapons. Look at the patterns here—indwelling animals, entering dreams, unwittingly serving God and fearing Him despite how powerful he becomes. He's not just a vampire. He may have used that form years ago, but that's not all he is. He's becoming something much, much worse. Whether a demon or something else, I don't know. But weapons will only slow him down; they won't kill him. He needs to be put to rest a certain way. And I think I understand it enough to do properly this time. *You* just have to trust me."

Christian tried to listen but stayed focused on the task at hand. "Alex, I love you like one of my own. But I can't let you do that. I couldn't live with myself if something happened to you. I'm not saying you're wrong or I don't trust you. I'm asking that you trust me enough to let me try it my way first. And if I fail, then I will be able to rest peacefully, knowing I gave it everything I could."

"But what about Rebecca and Adam? They need you."

"I know. But they'll understand. I'd rather die a hero than live as a tragedy. This is just something I have to do," he said, tearing up, knowing this might be the last time he saw her.

He kissed Alexandra on the forehead and left with droves of police cars and fire trucks behind him.

Alex wanted to stop him, but she understood Christian needed to find his peace in his own way and she should not interfere. She prayed quietly he did not die that night.

28

Huge Loss

A year prior, Alexandra had stood over Father Richard's body at his funeral. He looked like a molded piece of plastic—nothing like the man she remembered. Christian, Rebecca, and Adam crowded around her to give her hugs and support. They consoled her, but she was lost in her thoughts.

She was sad he died alone. Her mom was no longer there, and Alex had left him for the majority of those years during school when she could have been home more often, doing more to help him. He lived for his church and for the well-being of others, doing so many great things. He had taught her many lessons she'd never forget. And most important, he left the Catholic Church to marry her mother and have his family. She felt a vice around her heart, knowing she might never again experience a love and dedication that strong.

She looked at his face and wept not only for her loss but for her deep fear of dying in the same way.

"I'm so sorry, Daddy," she said under her breath, eyes glazed as she touched his stiffened arm. "I'm sorry I wasn't here for you more. I promise to make you proud of me. I won't forget any of it, and I will take care of these people for you. I love you so much. I'm going to miss you so terribly."

Rebecca embraced her, and Alex cried harder than she ever had before.

"You are capable, strong, and smart. You don't need anyone to complete you except God. Listen to your intuition and trust yourself," her father had told her as she grew up.

While she didn't know it at the time, she would need his words of wisdom as Blackheart returned to Meadowsville.

29

Brute Force

Christian stood in the broken, burned pieces of Blackheart's house. The last few firefighters were spraying holy water, taken from all the local churches, on the entire property. Christian hoped it would neutralize the blood of John Smith that permeated the soil. This was how he believed Blackheart stayed in his altered state after he was defeated by David and Christian. It preserved Blackheart's body in a way, possibly even strengthening it.

After eventually managing to escape from their station, every last police officer was also on the scene. They all waited for Blackheart. This was the town's last stand.

Christian walked the perimeter of the rubble, spreading gasoline like an animal marking his territory. He lit a match and dropped it down, igniting a blaze that turned the prior house into a ring of fire. He thought of his family and how

much he loved them, hopeful he would survive this battle—
and if he did not, that they would be proud of his sacrifice.
Beyond that, he would atone for the terrible things he'd done
over the last fifteen years.

He then heard children and realized Blackheart had put
all the missing children from town into the same room under
the house where Mr. Smith had kept Blackheart trapped
during most of his childhood.

The monster had felt a small amount of fear, knowing it
was using bait to give new life to his most feared nemesis, Mr.
Smith. But he was above the level of a mere vampire now. He
had become almost godlike.

The flames overwhelmed the children's cries, and Christian awaited the fight of his life. He put the thought of the
children out of his mind as his battle moved to the forefront.

Blackheart suddenly burst from the ground, arising from
the cement cellar mere feet away from Christian.

Christian didn't budge, unafraid of the monstrous
appearance.

Blackheart kicked the dirt and pieces of the house behind
him, blocking the hidden cellar door with all the children
inside. He prayed Smith would smell them and awaken.

"This time, you won't come back," Christian snarled.

All the cops had their guns ready but wouldn't fire for fear
of hitting Christian.

Blackheart and Christian walked toward each other,
neither showing any fear.

"I've waited fifteen long years for this."

"So have I," Blackheart growled. He smiled, spitting some of his polluted blood onto Christian's face, who scrambled to wipe it off.

Christian grabbed his ax and drove it into his enemy's ribcage as blood poured out. Christian flipped his hands up, moistened his gloves with holy water, and delivered thunderous blows to Blackheart, knocking him into the debris. He pulled out a knife and stabbed Blackheart in the shoulder, opening up the previously healed wound from Alexandra.

"Do you remember how this felt?" Christian called out, enjoying Blackheart's struggle. "Bleed for me."

Christian drank some of the holy water off his gloves and spit on Blackheart's face, disfiguring it more. He stood up and kicked him in the jaw. Blackheart squirmed on the ground as Christian towered over him.

Christian put one boot on the vampire's forearm and split it in two, exposing the bone. He took out his gun and shot Blackheart in the temple several times. With nothing left to prove, Christian moved to decapitate the monster with his ax. He admired the partial prayer on the ax: *I have not stopped giving thanks for you.*

Blackheart began laughing, which stopped Christian, now petrified of what was happening.

"What the hell is so funny?"

Blackheart stood up and began healing instantaneously. He took the exposed bone from his arm and pushed it out more, roaring with delight at the pain.

Christian was speechless and readied his ax again but wasn't sure what to do. Alexandra had been right. But now it was too late.

In an act of pure desperation, he began to swing the ax, but Blackheart used his exposed bone to slash Christian's thigh wide open, knocking him down to his knees. Blackheart kicked debris in Christian's face and stuck his fingers into the deep wound. Christian screamed so loudly he injured his throat.

Blackheart licked his hand and smiled, finally tasting the blood of his enemy. "You see. I learned a lot these past fifteen years. In that dirt. With Smith's blood keeping me here. Things I never fully understood before."

Christian writhed in pain, and Blackheart pulled his arm out of the socket, now keeping him flat on the ground.

"I become what you need me to be. And you can hurt me only when I allow you to. If you want a decent chance, then drink my blood. Be just like me. That's what you want," he said, cutting his own arm, trying to force it into Christian's mouth, but Christian resisted. Blackheart yanked off Christian's chest plate and left a bloody handprint on his shirt as a brand.

"But it doesn't matter now. Despite what you are, you can't kill me because I won't let you," Blackheart said, destroying the last of Christian's optimism.

He picked Christian up, tossing him into the air. Before he landed, Blackheart smashed a huge piece of wood across his now exposed chest. Christian spit up blood and tried pulling another knife out of his belt with his good arm. He heard the cries of dozens of children again as his hand sank into the remnants of the house, hitting the cement ceiling of the underground jail Mr. Smith had built for his victims. Christian regretted making them secondary to his ambitions in this battle, just as he'd done with his family all these years. He should have tried to save the children instead of fighting and focusing on his own needs.

"What are you going to do with them?" Christian mumbled, fighting the pain.

"Smith needs to feed. He loved the way we smelled. The odor of these things will help me give him new life. The process has already started. And when he's back, I'll finally have my chance to kill him the right way. My way. But only after he helps me destroy this place once and for all," Blackheart revealed. "I'll use him the same way he used me. And then I'll dispose of him and reach a new level. I will battle God, and I will destroy his finest creation, which is you wretched creatures."

Christian gasped at the thought of both Blackheart and Smith in Meadowsville together. He managed to get to his feet and balanced on the one uninjured leg, horrified at a biblical war being brought to the already heavily scarred town. He then prayed Alexandra had a strategy to sidetrack Blackheart's horrific ambitions.

"I'll die before I let you get that far," Christian declared.

"Christian, stay down. I will live forever. And I will terrorize your family for generations. And you can't stop me," Blackheart said, pushing Christian down with a single nudge.

Christian punched him with his last bit of energy, and it didn't faze Blackheart in the least. Christian stopped and let his body relax from its tensed state, realizing he should've listened to Alexandra. And he had once again abandoned his family for this monster. He deserved to die but would try to help with one last action. He signaled and yelled to the surrounding police and fire department crews that kids were trapped under the debris. The fire department quickly started extinguishing the blazing fire, and the police began shooting at Blackheart through the smoke, missing him with every shot. The sounds of the children became louder and louder.

Christian dropped to one knee as Blackheart viciously stomped his ankle sideways. He looked up at Blackheart, smiled in one last act of defiance, and readied himself to die. Blackheart grabbed Christian's shoes, using the flammable laces to light him on fire. He snapped Christian's hip out of place, lifted him up by the leg, and slammed him onto the cement, causing a nasty concussion and herniating several spinal discs. Blackheart pushed down on Christian's chest, using his prior handprint as a placeholder, crushing Christian's entire ribcage. He picked him up and pulled Christian, who tried desperately to breathe, right up to his face.

"Alexandra will be my greatest accomplishment. She will help me get to the Almighty. Thank you for gifting her to me."

With one mighty throw, he sent Christian hundreds of feet away into a deep thicket of thornbushes. Christian tried to extinguish the fire around his lower body but couldn't due to the injuries he had sustained, in addition to getting pricked by the thorns every time he moved. He passed out from the pain. Blackheart roared in victory and jumped into the night to find Alex. The police and fire personnel rushed through the debris and started digging, eventually finding all the children still safe. They then dowsed Christian in water, chopping at the thornbush to get him free. He was alive but sustained heavy injuries. They quickly began dressing his wounds and prepared to take him to Meadowsville Medical Center.

30

Alternate Strategy

Alexandra waited for Blackheart on the altar, dressed in a gorgeous white dress. Everyone in attendance at her earlier service was now gone. With a renewed sense of faith in both God and herself, she didn't feel alone. She stayed focused and harnessed all her energy into her plan. She quietly sang her favorite song to calm herself and bait him even more.

All the warnings, they were so clear
I still remember your grin when you ripped me apart
You deceived me from the start
It was all just a lie
I was too blind to see your dark intentions
Now we've reached the end
I thought you were my angel, in my time of need.

Blackheart landed by the front doors, shaking the entire building. He smashed through the front of the church and approached her quickly, hungrier than he'd ever been. His accompanying vultures stayed behind, almost guarding the entrance. This pure, virginal girl was all his now. A single tear fell down her face as she asked God to help her with this plan, and he licked it off with a disgusting notched tongue.

"I love how your tears taste," he said, awaiting his most anticipated kill. "You look so beautiful. All for me. I would never let Smith have you."

"I'm here for you and you alone," she said, fully engaging him.

He bit her, drinking several mouthfuls of blood, and she didn't try to stop him. The pain from it was like a dull ache. She said one more final prayer to God in hopes her idea worked.

Blackheart stopped, his body starting to burn from the inside. Alexandra had consumed a very large amount of holy water minutes before his arrival, knowing it would destroy him physically. He started to choke and dropped down to his knees before the altar, realizing he'd been tricked. The stained-glass eyes of Jesus lay on the floor before him. Watching him. Judging him. Alex put her hand over her neck, which had already started healing from the holy substance being so abundant. She did not absorb any of his blood. She was still herself. Blackheart hacked and dropped to his knees, almost as if being forced to kneel before God. His vultures were heard flying away, no longer under his control.

She looked at him, full of sadness. "God never forgot about you. He saved you. You were more important to him than anyone else. And he'll always love you," she whispered in his ear.

Blackheart looked at her with eyes showing his soul had just been freed, realizing the girl's wise words. He fell back and lay dying. Alexandra sat with him and held his limp hand. As the holy water continued to course through him, his blood vessels began to sink into his body, and his skin charred from the inside out. Alex was witnessing Blackheart experience his own personal hell on earth before her eyes. His death took several hours, and she sat with him the entire time. As the sun rose the next morning, it wasted away the last remaining parts of his body, sending his ashes out the windows of the church into the air, ascending into the skies. She smiled, feeling a deep sense of gratitude for being a critical part of Blackheart finding his final peace. All her life, she had trained for that moment, and it was as glorious and powerful as she had hoped. She was ready for anything and anyone now.

31

Rebuilding Meadowsville

onths later, Meadowsville worked on repairing itself from the damaging night when Blackheart was killed.

The parks and grounds supervisor, Johnny Mays, was temporarily reassigned and oversaw the cleanup at Blackheart's house on Chrysanthemum Drive. Between the animal carcasses and knocked-over trees, the work would take his crew weeks to clean up. They were ordered by Mayor Wiggins to not touch the remnants of the house or anything under the ground. While he couldn't bring himself to say it, there was still much uncertainty and unwillingness to learn just what was going on in that land. But they needed to repair the town before delving into that mystery. Wiggins also vowed to himself that he would never lie about his ambitions for the town ever again. As he reviewed estimates from his department heads to fix the damage done to the first responder buildings, he took a bottle of brandy out of his desk to help him process the outrageous costs involved.

"We may be broke, but at least we're honest." He laughed to himself.

The two residents who previously battled over their dogs laughed about it, shook hands, and exchanged pleasantries, allowing the dogs to mate before them now. What was once a massive ordeal was now downgraded to something for the men to joke about. Office Young coincidentally rolled by, waving at the two men, happy to see they'd put aside their differences, especially after the town's recent ordeal. Young pulled up to the police department, which was being fixed; of the four entrances, only one was currently accessible. He shook his head, smiled, and went inside to type a report.

Meadowsville High School also banned any Blackheart paraphernalia. Adam's teachers and classmates no longer teased him about his father's battles with the paranormal.

Church attendance was at an all-time high throughout town, especially at Meadowsville Community Church.

32

First Times

Christian, Rebecca, and Adam sat on a fresh wooden bench at Lucerne Lake before leaving to go to Alexandra's service that evening. The weather was fair, and Christian nuzzled his family, fully aware of his mistakes up to that point. He was determined to get better and be there for them. His first actions were seeking the right help. He was on new medications and felt more emotionally stable, seeing a new and better-suited therapist and psychiatrist, and accepting the therapeutic treatments as valuable aides. It was no longer about words but actions, and Christian now knew that. The reconciliation with Rebecca and Adam, both of whom were accepting of his apologies and drive to do better, was satisfying for the entire family.

They continued to sit lakeside and enjoy the view. *Lucerne* meant rebirth, and for the Reed family, that was exactly what this had become. Rebecca and Adam helped a heavily bandaged yet docile Christian up and into the car. Adam noticed a downed sign that read *Danger: high levels of hydrogen sulfide* near the lake. He wondered what the mild odor was and whether it would be dangerous for the residents around the lake.

Christian would also put away all of his weapons and armor, burying them in his junk-filled basement, hoping he'd truly seen the end of Blackheart. Much like his battle gear, he wanted to put that chapter of his life away for good. Now that he understood how the monster was a large part of his personal transformation over the last fifteen years, he would be able to choose a better future for himself and his family. He did have lingering questions on how Blackheart had planned to resurrect John Smith but hoped that was something the town would never have to encounter.

For the first time since Caroline's death, they visited her grave and wept together for their lost family member then entered Meadowsville Community Church to hear Alexandra's service.

Alexandra stood at the altar in the fully repaired church, preaching confidently to the congregation. She was indeed meant to be in this role. The doubt was no longer a barrier preventing her from being the adequate leader they needed her to be.

Adam, Rebecca, and Christian took their usual seats in the back pew. Several people patted Christian on the back gently, thanking him for his service as he limped in, using a cane and still nursing all his injuries from Blackheart.

Alex thought of how both Christian and she were right about what happened with Blackheart's attack. If it hadn't been for him engaging the monster in the way he chose to, those children would never have been found and saved and Mr. Smith might have been brought back. And if it hadn't been for her approach, Blackheart would have laid waste to the entire town by now. He would have killed her and taken over once and for all, continuing to test and judge the citizens in his own anarchic ways. No one else might have figured out the right way to finally defeat him simultaneously on physical, mental, and spiritual levels either. Now Christian and Alex had a complete and mutual respect that used to be a constant weak point between them. Rebecca gave her signature wink at Alex, who readied herself to speak.

"Glorious day, everyone. I want to take this time to speak on the biblical character Deborah. She wasn't mentioned much in the Bible, as she did not adhere to the cultural standards for women in that time. But she was a strong leader. The only female judge in Israel at the time, and a wife. In the book of judges, God's people veered away from spirituality and chose to worship other gods. When they eventually repented, God gave them strong leaders like Deborah. It seemed to be a divine appointment, as there are no records of her being formally put into the role through other means. And she was the only judge referred to as a prophetess, which reinforces the divine. She handled military strategies, administrative duties, and dispute settlements. She led an army with military leader Barak, who trusted she had the word of God. Under her, they overcame tremendous adversity, defeating larger and more able armies. God used her as a symbol. She didn't need to be revered, recognized, or praised. She was content being a servant of the Lord. She brought families, people, and nations back to God. And they were genuine. Israel then saw a time of extended peace."

She continued the sermon, content with her delivery and comparing Meadowsville and her own journey to this biblical figure, then concluded her homily. She had truly reached a new milestone and was ready for the next phase of her life—to lead this community, keeping them spiritually fulfilled and united against all future disturbances that might arise.

Because, deep down and much like Christian, she feared the return of John Smith, which Blackheart had almost deemed a certainty.

To be continued . . .

If you enjoyed *Preternatural Evolution*,
be sure to check out

PRETERNATURAL

RECKONING

This fast-paced adventure is a must-read for horror
aficionados and lovers of all things that are scary,
gruesome, and thought-provoking.